# —THE—
# STARLIGHT
# CLAIM

# TIM WYNNE-JONES

CANDLEWICK PRESS

*To all the Northenders, old and new*

Copyright © 2019 by Tim Wynne-Jones

Epigraph copyright © 2004 from *The Maestro* by Tim Wynne-Jones

First edition 2019

Library of Congress Catalog Card Number 2019939008
ISBN 978-1-5362-0264-9

19 20 21 22 23 24 LSC 10 9 8 7 6 5 4 3 2 1

Printed in Crawfordsville, IN, U.S.A.

This book was typeset in Minion Pro.

Candlewick Press
99 Dover Street
Somerville, Massachusetts 02144

visit us at www.candlewick.com

"I like the *idea* of winter," said the Maestro as he played. "I like the purity of it. I'm sure winter is the perfect cure."

"For what?" asked Burl. The Maestro didn't answer right away. He was caught up in a passage of music. Then he stopped.

"For everything," he said at last.

—from *The Maestro*

# 1

# The Dream

The dream was waiting for him. Dodge Hoebeek under a thick
sheet of crystal-clear ice, his eyes wide open, his fingers scraping at the glassy ceiling above him, his mouth screaming, bubbles
pouring out, and his long blond hair trailing behind him in the
black water.

Then somehow the streaming bubbles formed themselves into
words. "You gotta come, man! You owe me!" And Nate, kneeling
on the ice above his friend, his bare hands flat on the surface —
frozen to the surface — tried to speak but couldn't, as though he
were the one who was drowning.

"You owe me, Nate! It's your fault!"

"I'm sorry!" Nate shouted. "I'm so sorry!"

It was like he was looking into a warped carnival mirror,
unable to say anything, unable to do anything except throw his
head back and howl.

He woke up, his heart beating like a two-stroke engine. Had he really howled? He listened to the ticking stillness. No one was coming, so maybe not. Last fall he'd howled, good and loud. He'd woken, time and time again, with his head pressed to his mother's chest, her arms around him, his father standing just behind her, his hand on her shoulder, strong and calm.

"I've got to find him," Nate would say. And his mother would shush him. And he'd yell at her. "No! You don't understand. He needs me. He's waiting for me up there!" Eventually he would wear himself out. "It's all my fault," he'd say. "It's all my fault." His voice would grow hoarse and the tears would come and finally he'd lay his head back down on his pillow. His mother would fuss with the covers as if he were a five-year-old, touch her fingers to her lips and place them on his forehead, a benediction. Then she'd leave the room. But his father would stand there in the dark. Stand guard until he fell asleep. Stand there as long as it took.

# Escape

It was a daring escape. "Brazen escape," the TV anchorman called it. Nate watched as two jailbirds attempted to climb a knotted rope hanging from a helicopter.

"Is this for real?" said Nate. His father nodded, his eyes glued to the television. "So how come if they're filming it, nobody's trying to stop them?"

"CCTV," said his father.

Nate leaned against the doorjamb at the entrance to the den. It was late. He was in his pajama bottoms and a ratty Lockerby Vikings T-shirt. The men weren't getting very far on their climb toward the chopper. They were about as athletic as a couple of filing cabinets.

"Not exactly James Bond," said Nate.

His father chuckled.

The helicopter began to rise with the two guys hanging on for dear life. Up, up they rose toward the roofline of the jail that surrounded the yard on all four sides. The closed-circuit camera was in a fixed position, and soon enough the dangling criminals were whisked out of view. And then there was a new camera in play, the TV station camera, presumably, outside the jail. But there were no criminals or helicopter in sight, obviously. This was later. The camera was following the path the helicopter might have taken across a city covered in snow.

"Whoa!" said Nate as the scenery beyond the enclosed compound came into view. "Is that here?"

His father nodded. "The Sudbury Jail."

There were other shots of police roadblocks on various highways out of town, and then the news returned to the talking head with the frozen image of the escape on a screen behind him. Nate's dad pushed the mute button.

"I don't blame them one bit," he said.

"The convicts?"

"Uh-huh. That place is disgusting. Overcrowded, understaffed. And the mice? The place is completely infested."

Nate stared at his father. "Dad, is there something you want to tell me?"

His father held up his hands. "Busted," he said. "Yeah, I spent some time in the stony lonesome."

"Really?"

The grin gave him away. "Only as a visitor."

"Oh," said Nate, relieved but sort of disappointed. Burl Crow was the most decent, upstanding guy imaginable. It would be kind of cool if he had a shady past. Then again, maybe he did. "Visiting who?"

His father shook his head slowly, back and forth. He was looking toward the television but he had one of those thousand-yard stares on his face, the kind of blank, unfocused gaze of someone looking into the past. Then he snapped out of it.

"What are you doing up?" he said.

"Uh-uh," said Nate. "You're not getting off the hook that easy."

His father raised his eyebrows, trying to look parentally threatening but missing by a mile. Then he patted the couch next to him. Nate slouched into the room and sat down.

"My dad," said Burl. "Your grandfather."

"Oh, right." Nate had never met his grandfather, but he knew a bit about him. The burn on his father's right arm: that was thanks to Calvin Crow.

"What was he in for?"

His father laughed. "You name it. Arson for one thing, drunk and disorderly, aggravated assault, petty larceny — not-so-petty larceny."

"What's larceny?"

"Taking what isn't yours. That's my old man to a T." He put his hands together thoughtfully. "He was a thug, Nathaniel. Bad news."

"Did he die?"

"Haven't heard."

Nate frowned. "When was the last time you saw him?"

His father shrugged. "Five or six years ago, I guess. He was in for carjacking that time. He wanted me to bail him out and I had to draw the line. Not anymore. We're done."

He turned to Nate and tapped him on the knee. "What's up, son? I thought you went to bed an hour ago."

Nate let his head flop back onto the top of the couch. Closed his eyes.

"You want to tell me about it?" said his father.

"Not really," said Nate. It was old news. A jail he couldn't quite escape. "The dream," he said at last, trying to make it sound like no big deal.

"Again?"

"Uh-huh."

"I thought it had stopped."

Nate shook his head. His father waited. His father had an amazing capacity for waiting. He could wait out a rock. If you asked him about it, he'd say he learned it fishing.

"You think it's 'cause you're going up there?"

Nate sat up straight, yawned, pushed the hair out of his eyes. Felt a little dizzy for a moment. "I guess. Probably."

"You can always change your mind," said his father.

Nate shook his head. "Uh-uh," he said. He pursed his lips tight. Nothing would change his mind about going up to the lake. It had been in the cards for too long. Nate and Paul and Dodge. Except, no Dodge. Not now.

"You still planning on heading up Thursday?" Nate nodded. "Then you'd better get some shut-eye, kiddo. It's going to be hard slogging." Nate nodded again. "There'll probably be two or three feet of snow on the trail."

"I know, Dad. It's cool."

"More like minus twenty."

Nate scowled at his father. "Are you seriously trying to talk me out of this?"

His father held his gaze for a moment. "Do you think I'd stand a chance?"

Nate could see the hint of a smile. Shook his head. Then his father ruffled his hair. "Git," he said.

Nate pushed his father's hand away but then held on to it a moment. His father's hands were strong, brown even in the dead of winter. He could see the burn on his forearm, poking out under the rolled-up cuff of his shirt. A place where no hair grew, grizzled. Fried.

"How'd he take it?" asked Nate.

There was a pause while his dad figured out what Nate was talking about. "My old man?" Nate nodded. His father looked thoughtful. "Calvin Crow is used to *taking* only what he wants. He doesn't like being crossed, and he sure let me know it. All I could do was let him rant and shout and punch a hole in the wall — or try to. Then he clammed up. I left without a goodbye from him. And that was that."

Nate thought about it, tried to imagine turning down your father's plea for help. Couldn't. "What'd you call it? The 'stony lonesome'?"

His father smiled. "Git," he said again.

The front door opened and closed: Mom, home from her night class.

Nate looked at the watch on his father's arm. "She's late," he said, climbing to his feet, yawning, stretching.

"Probably out on a pub crawl with her twenty-something classmates."

They both laughed at that. They were still laughing when Astrid appeared at the den doorway. "What are you two up to?" she said.

"We were talking about your drinking problem," said Nate. He hugged his mother and got as good as he gave.

"Right about now my drinking problem might stretch to a cup of herbal tea. Anybody else?"

So the three of them made their way to the kitchen. It was March break — spring break for folks in warmer climes. Sudbury was still serving out its sentence for being north of the forty-sixth parallel. The days were longer, but winter was hanging on tight. Burl put the kettle on the stove, Nate got out the cups, and Astrid set out a plate of jam-filled thumbprint cookies on the table while she talked about all the fun stuff she'd learned in Vibrations and Dynamic Systems. His parents had both been high-school teachers; Burl still was, but Astrid quit and was in her last year of studying mechanical engineering.

Astrid Ekholm was as blond as Nate's father was dark. And Nate was a little bit of all they were: almond-shaped eyes like his father's but glacial blue like his mom's; his father's straight hair but some in-between color. "Hey, Doc Savage," Dodge had called him not long after they met. Nate had shrugged it off. "At least I'm not named after a car," he'd said. And Dodge had said, "A truck. I'm named after a truck." And that was that.

"How was the party?" said his mother, pouring him a cup of Sleepytime.

Nate snapped out of his thoughts. "I didn't go."

His mother stopped pouring. "Aren't you feeling well?"

He shrugged, dolloped honey into the steaming cup. "No, I just . . . I had a bad feeling it was going to get dicey."

His mother turned to his father, who held up his hands in wonder. "Let me see if I've got this right," said Astrid. "It's March break and my newly sixteen-year-old son decides not to go to a party because it might get 'dicey' — was that what you said?"

Nate sighed, showily, to make his exasperation clear. "Jason's parents are out of town. The party was all over the school — it'd gone viral. There were going to be like a million people there—guys crashing from all over and . . ." He twirled his finger in the air and made a sound like a police siren. "Who needs it?"

His mother nodded slowly. "Did either of us tell you lately you're an amazing son?"

Nate appeared to give it some serious thought. Then he nodded. "Yeah. All the time."

# For the Rest of Your Death

"It's a crazy idea, Art. . . . No, seriously. I can't object more strenuously."

Burl is on the phone. Early last November. Nate seldom hears his father raise his voice, although if anybody could wear his patience thin, Art Hoebeek was the one to do it.

Nate waits, watches his father rub his forehead with his thumb and forefinger. He and Art back-and-forth a bit and finally the call ends. "What was that about?" says Nate.

Burl takes a deep breath. "Art's got another harebrained scheme," he says. "He's found this secondhand propane refrigerator in 'mint condition' and he wants to bring it up to the camp. Now. Says he's going to spring Dodge and Trick from school to help out."

For a fraction of a moment Nate is elated. The Hoebeeks live in Indiana; he gets to see Dodge all summer but seldom after

Canadian Thanksgiving. But the consternation on his father's face brings him up short.

"So what's harebrained about it, exactly?" he asks. His father gives him the look that means *work it out.* "Okay," says Nate. "So if they bring it up on the Budd car, they'd have to truck it in from the track on the Mule." His father raises an eyebrow. Nate thinks. "Is the Mule's cargo bay big enough to handle a fridge?" His father nods. "But it's a propane fridge, right? So basically, you try to cart it in on the trail, it's going to be scrap metal."

His father holds up a hand. "The fridge is sturdy enough. The big problem is the risk of shaking loose scale in the cooling tubes—"

"Yeah, yeah, yeah," says Nate, seeing a TED Talk coming on. "Bottom line, the trail is murder if you could even use it now. I mean, if there's snow up there . . ." Another nod. *Keep going.* Nate clenches his teeth and resists growling. His friends' fathers tend to have all the answers right on the tips of their tongues. Nate knows that his own father has the answers, all right, but he keeps his tongue inside his head. *Work it out, Nate.* "Okay, so . . . Oh!" He slaps himself on the forehead. "He's not going to come in from Mile Thirty-Nine; he's planning to get off at Southend and bring it up the lake?"

"Got it," said Burl.

"Won't it be frozen by now?"

His father shrugs. "It's been a warm fall. I doubt it. But the water will be pretty darn close to freezing, in any case."

Nate thinks about it. He'd been up to the lake at least once in every month of the year. You didn't go in the water after September if you could avoid it, and you got out quick if you did. "So why doesn't he just wait for it to freeze solid and then we could drag it in with the snowmobile?"

"Bingo," says Burl. "That's what I tried to tell him. But he's dying to get up there again before winter sets in, because of having to miss close-up."

That was the usual way of things. The two families met at Ghost Lake the second weekend of October and had one last big meal together, then closed the two camps up good and tight: boarded up the windows, shut down the pumps, put away the boats, et cetera. But this year had been different. Mr. H. was a big-deal pharmaceutical salesman, and a medical conference had come up, something he couldn't miss. The Crows had offered to close up the Hoebeek camp for them, but Art had declined the offer because he was going to get there "by hook or by crook." That's what he'd said. Which, at the time, had not seemed such a big deal. If they were just going to come up on the Budd car to Mile 39, where the trail led into the north end of the lake, it would be fine. It might be wet, it might be cold; there might even be snow but not too much, not this November. In fact, the idea had sounded great to Nate back then. He'd planned to go along.

But the fridge changed all that.

So the plan, it turned out, was to get off the train at Southend, which was more than twenty kilometers down the lake.

"What's that in real people's language?" Art Hoebeek would have said.

"About twelve and a half miles, Art," Burl would have answered him, knowing full well that Art knew the distance to the end of the lake. "You're going to have to take it real slow and stay as close to the shore as you can, just in case. With a weight like that and the three of you on board . . . it could be dark before you make it in. I don't like it one bit."

But Mr. H. was determined. And Burl had backed down.

"He's a grown man," Burl had said to Nate. "What are you going to do?"

A grown man but an idiot as far as Nate was concerned.

Later, when the whole story came out, or as much as anybody would ever be able to piece together, they learned Art had asked Likely La Cloche if he and the boys could borrow his sixteen-foot aluminum utility boat. Likely was an old-timer, a Ghost Lake icon. Nate didn't know his real name. Burl told him that he was called Likely because if you thought you'd discovered something new about the lake, it was likely that old Monsieur La Cloche already knew about it. He lived at Sanctuary Cove down near Southend most of the fall. There was a whole busy little community of folks at Sanctuary, thirty or forty camps' worth, that Nate hardly ever saw, except the odd boatload of anglers who came up the lake to troll for trout between the islands. Likely had said, sure, Art could borrow the boat. What Art had failed to tell him was that he was bringing a fridge.

"Why would Likely let them do that?" Burl had said when he first heard about the accident. Turned out Likely reneged on his offer when he saw the fridge. Said they could store it with him in his shed and take it in next summer. "So what happened?"

Burl's forehead had crinkled up and he'd looked away.

"Dad?"

"I guess Art must have turned on his salesman's charm." Nate had nodded. "You know what he's like. The weather's calm, the lake placid, the sun bright in a cloudless sky. A beautiful late fall day. What could happen?"

They had found the boat overturned in Dead Horse Bay.

They had found Art Hoebeek and Trick, Dodge's twelve-year-old brother, floating in their PFDs just the way they ought to be, face up, arms out. No chance of drowning in a personal flotation device. They hadn't drowned; they were dead from hypothermia.

The search party never did find Dodge.

Burl Crow had gone up that awful November day they got the news, but he wouldn't let Nate come along. They had fought about it. Or, at least, Nate fought, and Burl just waited him out. There had hardly ever been a time he'd said no to his son about going with him to the lake. Just once before, really, a week earlier when Dodge had asked him to come along on the fridge expedition. Nate had stomped to his room and slammed the door. That was a first, too.

The search party had been cut short by the first big snowstorm of the season. It had raged for three days. By the end of it, the snow was thick on the ground and the ice was forming on Ghost Lake. There was no other way into Dead Horse Bay. There was deep forest right down to the waterfront. Another search party had gone up anyway, tried to hack their way in from the trail at the dam, but with no luck.

Dodge was still out there.

A year ago, eight months before the fatal trip, the three boys — Nate, Dodge, and Paul — had gone up to Ghost Lake with Burl over March break. It was a test. If the boys passed, they could go up alone next March. It was next March now. But it was going to be just Nate and his friend from school, Paul Jokinen, heading up on Thursday.

"You sure about this?"

"Yeah."

His father nodded. Waited.

"What?"

"Have you got some idea about looking for him?"

Nate's eyes skittered away from his father's. But you didn't lie to Burl. There was no point in it. So he nodded.

"The lake's frozen solid, Nate. Probably ten inches thick. There'll be a ton of snow."

"I know."

"Are you planning anything foolish?" Burl asked.

Nate shook his head, hurt by the implications. "I'm not stupid," he said. His father nodded. Waited. "Maybe we'll poke around along the shoreline of Dead Horse. Check out the east side of Picnic Island. You know, in case the current shifted . . ." It wasn't really a plan; it was more like a deep-seated need to do something — *anything*.

Then his father laid his strong hands on Nate's shoulders. "There's nothing you could have done, Nathaniel."

Nate looked into his father's eyes. "He pleaded with me to go."

"I know."

"If I'd been there, Dad, I wouldn't have let it happen. I'd have stopped them."

"I believe that. Or I believe you'd have tried. But Art Hoebeek . . . he was —"

"An idiot?"

His father frowned. "I was going to say a difficult man to convince when he had an idea in his head."

"I'll never forgive him," said Nate. Then he bowed his head. He'd never forgive himself either, and his father knew it. They'd been all over that.

His father didn't pass judgment. His mind was focused on Nate and Paul's upcoming trip. "Nate?" He looked up. "You die out there, son, I'm going to get real angry." Nate smiled, but his father didn't smile back. "You have no idea," he said, shaking his head. "Hell, I'll be angry with you for the rest of your death."

Gallows humor. Nate laughed, but it caught in his throat. His father wasn't being funny. And the line stayed with Nate. *I'll be angry with you for the rest of your death.* That was not a fate he wanted to face.

Burl Crow was a teacher by avocation and training, a guidance counselor by profession. But in the bush, he didn't teach so much as showed and waited. He had expected his three students to ask before they screwed up, rather than warning them beforehand. Think first, that was the crucial thing in the wild.

They had gone over the Ski-Doo, troubleshooting. It was an old model Burl kept in excellent condition. It wasn't enough to be able to operate it, as far as he was concerned; you had to treat it tenderly and know what to do when it stopped dead in the middle of nowhere. The Hoebeeks had a new-model Polaris, less likely to cause any trouble. Dodge knew the Polaris just fine, so Burl made him conduct a workshop on its finer points. Dodge hadn't much liked being schooled, but he loved being the center of attention. He had hammed it up, big time. But he knew his stuff and that was all Burl wanted to know.

Thorough. Nate's father was all about thorough.

The three boys had learned how to safely climb on the roof and shovel off the solar panels so they could have enough electricity for lights, the radio, charging their cell phones. Not that there was any reception, not so much as a single bar — not at water level, anyway. But up behind the camp, high on a cliff overlooking the lake, there was an abandoned shack that a miner had built ages ago. His name was Japheth Starlight, and the Crow camp stood on the old Starlight claim. Nate had never met Starlight. He was long since dead and gone. But his tiny, perfect shack was still there and Burl had kept it shipshape, repairing major bear damage on one occasion, propping it up when it started to list with age. From up there, you could get reception.

"First sign of any trouble . . ."

Dodge had pulled out his cell phone. "Up the hill," he had said. They all knew the drill. There had been blazes carved on the trees to show the path up to the shack. Burl had the trio find their way up by themselves while he waited below. They tied plastic orange ribbons on branches where the old tree blazes had grown dull with age. Nate had texted his mother from the cliff top. "The eagle has landed," he wrote. He'd watched for almost a minute until the "delivered" notification popped up. He'd wanted to wait for her to reply but Dodge was impatient, so they'd made their way down the hill back to the camp with Dodge out front leading the way. Nate could still see — would always see — Dodge tramping down that hill through the bush, pulling ahead of him and Paul. Because that's what Dodge did. He was always on to the next thing, one step ahead of you. Now, in Nate's imagining, Dodge pulled farther and farther ahead until he disappeared into the bush. Just walked right into the next world, wherever that was.

He would never be dead to Nate until there was a body. Dodge was up there somewhere. And if anyone could find him, it would be Nate.

# The Numbster

You've got to come.

Can't.

Dude!!!

The Mighty Burl has spoken. Too dangerous.

Hold that thought . . .

Nate is still sitting on his bed with the cell phone in his hands, punching out a text, when Dodge phones.

"It *won't* be too dangerous if *you* come," he says without introduction.

"What does that mean?" says Nate.

"Dad thinks you're smart. He obviously doesn't know you as well as I do, but he'll listen to you, man."

"Hah!" The laugh erupts from Nate. "You don't listen to me; why would your father?"

"Because he thinks you've got this, I don't know, deep-woods Canadian wisdom. . . . You know . . ."

Nate isn't sure if Dodge is messing with him. "What's that supposed to mean?"

"Oh, come on, man. You know what I'm saying. Like your dad."

And suddenly Nate feels uncomfortable, as if Dodge is saying something that's only sort of a compliment but is something else as well. Something that is always there with Dodge. Their *difference*. Nate is never just Nate to him. He's a category. The other.

"You still there?"

"Yeah. I'm just wondering why you're such a dick."

"Forget about it," says Dodge. "All I'm *really* saying is that if you're along for the ride, nothing bad will happen."

"Like I'm a lucky rabbit's foot?"

Dodge groans with frustration. "Just say yes, Numbster. It'll be cool."

Nate changes the subject. Asks about school, how the Wildcats' season is going, whether Dodge asked that girl out.

"Which one?"

"The cheerleader."

"Cindi? Man, that is so last week."

And so on. The appeal to Nate — the demand — is dropped, but he can tell that Dodge is pissed. Then someone calls Dodge to the dinner table and he says goodbye, just like that.

"I wish you weren't going up there," says Nate. But the line is already dead.

And then, two weeks later, Dodge is dead. His father is dead, and skinny little Patrick, always with the puffer for his asthma, is dead. And Nate can't help thinking if he'd been there, maybe it wouldn't have happened. Maybe Art Hoebeek would have listened to him. Right.

There is an e-mail from Dodge, two days before the Hoebeeks set off from Indiana.

Numbster—I mean Nate the Great—this is your last chance! The once-in-a-lifetime offer is still on the table. A chance to hang out with the one and only Dodge Hoebeek one mo' time before the winter sets in. Seriously, man, here's the deal. Dad knows the weather could get bad. He's got a backup plan. We get there and if it's lousy, we leave the fridge at Sanctuary Cove with old man La Cloche. We stay there the night, take the Budd back to Sudbury the next day. We don't do the big fridge thing unless it's perfect, right? So come on. Deal?

# The Lie

He didn't usually sleep in, but it was eleven when Nate got up Wednesday morning. He woke to the house phone ringing. He checked his cell and saw there was a missed message. Paul.

"I'm up," he called down to his mother when he heard her answering the phone. She appeared at the bottom of the stairs with the cordless in her hand.

"Paul," she said, her hand over the receiver. She was frowning.

"What's up?"

"He doesn't sound so hot."

Nate took the phone, gulping down his foreboding. He went back to his room, closing the door behind him.

"Hey," he said.

"I called you at, like, nine."

"Yeah, well I was dead to the world. Bad night."

"Tell me about it."

"This doesn't sound good."

There was a pause at the end of the line as big as the northern tundra. "I can't go," said Paul.

Nate couldn't think of what to say.

"I'm sorry, man. Really."

More silence.

"Talk to me, Nate."

"What the —"

"I'm grounded," said Paul. Nate looked out at the snow, squinting at the brightness, trying to tamp down his anger. "And don't remind me you said not to go to the fricking party."

"You went to the fricking party?"

"I said don't remind me."

"Paul —"

"I know, I know."

Nate lowered his voice. "Paul, I can't go without —"

"I said *I know* Nate. You can't go to camp unless I go, too. Got it, for Christ's sake! Don't rub it in."

"Jeezus!"

There was a long pause. "Sorry," Paul mumbled.

Nate took a deep breath. He checked to see that he'd shut the door. The plan was dissolving before his eyes, swirling into nothing just like the snow squalls outside his window.

"We've been talking about this trip for months — all year!"

"I said I'm sorry."

Nate sighed. "I heard you."

"My folks are, like, through the roof."

"What happened?"

"Beer pong is what happened."

Nate was thinking hard. "Could I talk to them?" he asked.

"My parents?"

"No, the Jedi Knights."

"Well, you'd have about as much chance of talking to the Jedi Knights as to my parents. Man, I got so loaded." He groaned. "I know—I'm a douche bag. A total fricking douche bag. And if it makes you feel better, I feel like death warmed over."

Nate sat down on the edge of his bed. It did make him feel better, but only marginally.

"Like I said, I owe you, big time."

Nate closed his eyes, counted to five, slowly in three languages. "Okay."

"So . . . you accept my apology?"

"No way. I'm writing down what you said about owing me big time."

At the other end, someone was speaking to Paul, his mother, by the sound of it. "That was my jail guard," he said mournfully. "I've got to get off the phone. See you, okay? Once I get out."

"Like in five years?"

"Maybe I'll get early parole if I load the dishwasher."

Nate smiled, despite everything. "Maybe I could bust you out," he said.

"Yeah, get the *Mission Impossible* team back together."

Nate managed a halfhearted laugh. Actually, he'd been thinking of a helicopter and a rope with knots in it. "See you," he said.

"Yeah."

*Click.*

Nate pushed the off button and chucked the cordless onto the bed beside him. He stood up, crossed the room to the window, and leaned on the sill. The temperature had dipped to minus twenty-five Centigrade.

"That would be minus thirteen, to you, Mr. H.," he muttered to himself.

The sun was dazzling. Ah, March in Northern Ontario. It was snow-globe stuff outside, not a real snowfall.

There was a knock on his door.

"Yeah?"

Mom poked her head in. "Is he okay?"

"Uh, yeah," said Nate, wiping the gloomy look off his face. "He just has a headache."

His mother stared at him. "So everything's still on?"

The pause before Nate spoke was little more than a nanosecond. "Yeah," he said, sticking both thumbs in the air.

"Good," said Astrid. "This is going to be so exciting, right?"

"Right," said Nate. "I can hardly wait."

There were only two ways into Ghost Lake: a plane or the Budd car. The Budd was a diesel train, usually two cars long, that traveled from Sudbury northwest to White River. It went up one day and down the next, with no service on Monday. It made a handful of scheduled stops along the way, but you could get the engineer to stop anywhere you liked. The trail into the camp at Ghost Lake was at Mile 39 out of Pharaoh, about three hours north of Sudbury. The camp was a two-kilometer hike from the track, or a mile and a half in Hoebeek. But however you measured it, the hike in was a long one, carrying everything you needed on your back. Which is what it came down to in winter when the Kawasaki Mule was shut up tight in its shed. There was emergency grub at the camp, dry goods and cans. But basically, you carried everything in or did without. If you were staying for any length of time, you could come back to the track with the snowmobile, but that was for wusses.

Nate shook his head. He *should* have gone to the damn party. He could have kept Paul on the up and up. Reminded him about Thursday. Dragged him home —

"So have you made up your mind?"

Nate looked up. Astrid was smiling at him from behind a loaded grocery cart. He was standing in the canned food aisle with two different brands of beef stew in his hands. "Yeah, pretty much," he said. He was going to put one can back on the shelf and then remembered he was shopping for two. He put them both in the cart. There was food there for four days, for two teenage boys.

His mother frowned. "When you get back I'm putting you on a strict diet of fresh vegetables and fruit," she said, shaking her head at the contents of the cart. Nate summoned up a smile that wouldn't have registered above 2.5 on any kind of smile-o-meter.

His mother's frown deepened.

"What?" he said.

"Is something wrong, Nate?" she said.

"No. Why?"

"Are you getting cold feet?" He shook his head. "Because you can always change your mind."

"What is this? First Dad and now you."

She held up her hands in surrender. "Just checking."

For one moment he thought he'd break down and confess. But then there was Dodge in his head whispering to him.

*You've got to come, Numbster. You owe me.*

"I guess I'm just a little nervous," he said.

"It's a big deal," said Astrid, "without your father along and all."

"Yeah," he said.

"Nate, you don't have anything to prove."

"Right," he said. "Of course." But that was also a lie.

He glared at the pile of groceries he'd be carrying in himself. Could he do it in one trip? All those hills. All that snow. Alone.

"I'm good," he said.

Astrid reached out, cupped his chin like he was a child, made him look into her eyes. Another shopper walked by, staring at him surreptitiously, as if he were about to get scolded. He concentrated his gaze on his mother; it took every muscle in his body. She wasn't exactly a mind reader, but there was no fooling her. He must have passed the test. She smiled. "Well, let's get this stuff home. Early night, right?"

"Right," he said. He even managed a smile. He was a better liar than he'd have ever guessed. The idea didn't give him much comfort.

# The Budd and Beyond

Astrid had a class field trip to a power plant Thursday morning, so she was going to be up and out early. Dad was going to drop Nate off at the train station on his way to school. It may have been March break for the students, but his father was on some kind of planning committee.

"We picking up Paul?" he asked.

"Nah, his dad's going to drop him off." Nate stared straight ahead. The lying wasn't getting any easier.

"Nervous?" said Burl.

"Mostly just excited," said Nate, and a little chunk of him broke off inside, like an iceberg calving into his bloodstream.

The Budd left at nine if it was on time, which it seldom was. There weren't many passengers this time of year. In summer, there might be scores of them, troops of Boy Scouts and gaggles of trippers, a dozen canoes to load, lumber for construction, sometimes an ATV. This time of year, there'd be a handful of intrepid souls, the odd trapper, or maybe somebody's grandmother heading all the way to the end of the line.

Burl looked at the time on his wristwatch, looked up and down the platform.

"Just go, Dad," said Nate. "You know Paul. He's always last minute."

His father clapped him on the shoulder. "Got it."

"You're more nervous than me," said Nate. "You shouldn't be."

His father relaxed his shoulders. "Okay. You're right. You guys are going to be fine." He looked up at the enamel-blue sky. "The weather should be okay going in. There's a storm coming, but not until Saturday. Might mean a long wait coming out on Sunday."

"Like that's never happened?"

"Right," said his father. "Okay, I'm off. Send a text when you get a chance."

"I'll send Mom a text. You never even look at your cell."

Burl smiled.

*Just go! Please, before the truth leaks out of me all over the damn platform.*

Then his father was gone and part of Nate wished Burl had seen through him. Paul sometimes joked about how Nate was the only kid he knew whose parents trusted him. "What's that like?" he'd say. Well, right now it was horrible.

"Going it alone?"

Nate turned. It was Gabriel, the baggage hand.

"Yeah. First time."

"You hear about the storm?"

"Saturday, right?"

Gabriel grabbed the Woods No. 1 Special pack and hoisted it onto the baggage car. The Woods pack was old-school: canvas and leather, designed to hold the front quarter of a moose. "When you coming out?"

"Sunday. And yeah, I know it might be a long wait."

Gabriel smiled. "Well, you won't go hungry, eh?" he said, wiping his brow as if the pack weighed a ton.

Nate handed up his snowshoes and poles — big old ski poles with wide powder baskets at the bottom. Gabe placed the gear beside the Woods pack on the floor of the otherwise empty baggage car. "Mile Thirty-Nine, right?"

"You got it."

"We should be leaving in five," said Gabriel.

"Excellent," said Nate. Then he turned to look back through the glass doors into the station, hoping to see Paul at the ticket office waving at him: a last-minute reprieve — a stay of execution. "Let's do this thing!" he imagined Paul saying. But there was no one in the ticket line, no one in the whole station except for a couple of employees behind the counter, yukking it up.

He was on his own.

Towering rock and endless, marching troops of trees, interrupted by glimpses of a pure-white fastness: a sleeping lake, a river. The Boreal forest "made out of chaos and old night." It was a line from some writer his father liked. Endless tracts of bush and ragged, jutting granite: the Precambrian shield, the oldest mountain range in the world, worn down over millennia, glistening with snowmelt that had frozen into sheets of ice, blinding in the high, bright sun.

The earth was still winter deep, but the sun in the wheeling blue sky didn't know it. Sol wouldn't set until seven-thirty or so. There'd be plenty of time to trek in and trek back on foot for a second load if he felt like he had to divide up what was in the Woods pack. He'd emptied the canned goods into double Ziploc bags and put them, the frozen meat, and bags of frozen vegetables into a cooler. Not that it needed keeping cool. The idea was that if he couldn't manage the weight of the pack, he could leave the cooler at the head of the trail and come back for it. By snowshoe, if he didn't feel like digging out the doors to the Ski-Doo shed. He almost thought he'd prefer two trips on foot. He liked the old snowmobile well enough, especially out on the lake doing dough-nuts while Dodge raced circles around him in his more powerful machine. But he had this whole kind of ritualistic thing he liked about getting there under his own steam — doing the "man thing," as Dodge called it. Going up to camp wasn't the same to folks in the south, driving up to their cottage door, switching on the power. You had this train to catch, first off, and then a hard slog on the trail, where there was a lot more up than down, at least on the way in. You were only truly there when you had everything you needed in the camp — and a fire started to melt the hoar-frost off the inside walls. After that, Nate liked to take a good long minute to stand, mission accomplished, looking out at the lake. It seemed particularly apt on this, his first solo effort. Doing it on foot might even help to work off some of the guilt that churned inside him.

How guilty had he looked back at the train station? Had his dad picked up on it? All it would take would be a call to the Jokinens. There would still be cell communication for a couple of hours or more. But by the time the train stopped at Presqueville, an hour out of Sudbury, his phone hadn't rung. He'd checked it more than once, made sure it was charged, made sure the ringer was on.

Presqueville was where Burl had lived after he ran away from his father's abuse and his mother's drug-induced stupor. He'd worked for a bush pilot awhile, then stayed with the Agnew family all the way through high school before he went to university. They still saw Auntie Natalie and Uncle Dave every Christmas.

Burl had run away and found a kind of a home on Ghost Lake before Cal burned it down. That was a whole other story. Then Burl had found a real home with the Agnews, where he had begun a new life. They were the only family his father had, as far as Nate knew.

Astrid, on the other hand, came complete with a big, warm Scandinavian family of three large brothers, a sister, and two parents still very much alive. The Ekholms gave him cousins; the Crows gave him mystery.

An hour out of Presqueville, the Budd pulled into Pharaoh, with its rows and rows of tracks. There were more freight cars in Pharaoh on any given day than there were people. It was near here, out in the boonies, that his father had been born and lived until he was fifteen. Nate had never thought of it before, but in going up to Ghost Lake it was as if he were traveling backward through his father's life. He rested his forehead against the cold window, looking out across the tracks. He was slipping into a sadness he couldn't afford right now. His father had run away from home for his own survival. And here was Nate running away from . . . from what? From the most loving and perfect parents you could ever hope for. What was he doing?

"We're going to be tied up for a bit."

Nate looked up to see the new, cheery conductor lady, whose name he didn't remember. "We're so delayed, we timed out," she said. She must have seen the confusion on Nate's face, so she explained about government regulations and waiting for a new crew. She shook her head and shrugged. "What can you do?"

"Yeah. What can you do."

"Can I get you anything? A coffee, soup, chips?"

"No thanks," said Nate.

She moved along, and when she was gone he palmed the cell phone in his parka pocket. He could end it all here. He didn't have to wait to be found out. He could just phone home.

"I lied. Paul couldn't come. Can you pick me up?"

Pharaoh was the last place you could get to by car when you were heading up to the lake. He knew his father would come for him. If he was in a meeting, Nate might have to wait. But Burl would show up as soon as he could. There'd be no recriminations. His father wasn't built that way. There would be no yelling. No grounding. No docking of allowance. That wasn't the way things worked in the Ekholm-Crow household. The punishment was no punishment at all.

A freight train pulled into the station, going about the speed of a snail on tranqs. Too noisy to make a call now, he thought.

*You've got to come, Numbster. You owe me.*

Numbster. Short for numb nuts. Dodge had been a sentimental guy.

"What am I going to call you?" says Dodge. He hurls the hardball. Nate nabs it, hurls it back.

"How about Nate?"

"Yeah, yeah, yeah, but you gotta have a handle."

*Smack.* The ball hits the pocket of Nate's glove. He digs it out and throws a high one into the sun.

"I don't know," says Nate, watching Dodge shield his eyes and snag the pop-up at the last second. "You could call me Igniculus the Firefly, if you like."

"Bah!" says Dodge. *Smack.* "Something better."

Nate smiles. "How about . . . Oh, I know: Nate."

Dodge throws a mean grounder that takes a bad bounce and

hits Nate in the chest. Dodge laughs. "Error, error. Runner totally safe at first."

Nate puts extra mustard on his return throw and watches Dodge hide behind his glove. Nate's turn to laugh. Dodge hurls the ball back.

"Hey, I got it," he says. "I'm going to call you Cleveland."

Nate stares at him. "Cleveland?"

"Yeah," says Dodge, lobbing the ball back. "You know."

Nate doesn't know, but when the ball lands in his mitt the penny drops. "No way," he says.

"Oh, come on," says Dodge. "It's perfect. I love it."

Nate looks at the scuffed-up ball in his hand, finds the seam. A knuckleball is called for.

"Ouch!" says Dodge as the ball caroms off his mitt and lands in the bushes by the water. "Take it easy, Cleveland."

By the time he digs the ball out and turns to look, Nate is walking back toward his camp. "Hey," he yells. "What's your problem?"

Nate doesn't bother to answer. They've been thrown together and mostly it's great, but some days, Nate finds Dodge too much.

"Okay, okay, okay!" yells Dodge. "I won't call you Cleveland." Nate stops but doesn't turn around. "How about Numb Nuts?" says Dodge. Nate throws his mitt to the ground and takes off after Dodge, who's already discarded his own mitt and is heading out into the lake, laughing his head off. A battle royal is about to take place, involving such instruments of destruction as pool noodles and wet T-shirts. There will be much laughter and never another mention of Cleveland.

No call came. Nate willed the phone to ring. His parents trusted him. Which only made it worse. By the time the slow freight train had gone and the new crew had arrived and the Budd finally pulled out of Pharaoh and crossed the Timmins Highway, it was going on one o'clock. He pulled out his cell phone one last time. No bars. No chance to change anything now.

Gabriel handed down the Woods pack. The snow was always deepest ten feet to either side of the tracks, where the plow dumped it. Nate had wrestled his way from the passenger car to the baggage car in snow up to his crotch. Gabriel had handed down the snowshoes first and Nate placed the heavy Woods pack on the snowshoes, which sunk an inch or two under its weight.

"Out on Sunday, right?" shouted Gabriel over the gasping of the brakes and the rattle of the idling engine. Nate craned his neck up at him, nodded. "See you then, eh? Have a good one."

Nate saluted and then fought his way back from the tracks. Gabriel was on the walkie-talkie to the engineer. Soon enough the bell rang and the engine picked up steam. The Budd was on its way, north by northwest. Catching his breath, Nate watched it round the next bend until there was nothing left of it but sound. And after that, the sound of the true north closed in around him, the wind and the shooshing of the tall trees and the raucous shout of a raven out hunting for a meal, in the shining sky.

He was alone. The deal was sealed.

The first hill was the worst. It wasn't all that long, but it was steep and rocky, and his father, determined to keep the trailhead secret, never cut it back much, so you got your face slapped a whole lot by whippy branches as you carted stuff up the hill. It was only twice as hard in snowshoes.

When he got to the top, he broke out a bottle of water and pretty much downed the whole thing. Despite the sun beating down, it was minus fifteen or so, and that would be the day's high. He knew for sure now that he'd have to make a second trip from the camp. He took out the cooler and strapped it shut. At this time of year, the bears were hibernating, so you didn't have to worry too much about leaving a container full of food at the trail-head. In summer, they'd douse the cooler with bleach, just to be sure. Still, it was hard to leave it. He felt nervous for some reason. The guilts again. Was he going to feel like this for the next three days? He shook his head angrily. Then he took a deep nose-hair-stinging breath and set off. He was glad of the big baskets on the ski poles — the snow was powder, soft and deep.

After that opening hill from the train bed, there were three major climbs. Dodge had named them as if they were a series of horror movies: *Everest, Killer Everest,* and *Everest — the Return.* The weird thing is that the way was actually easier in winter because there were no rocks and not as much vegetation swatting you left and right. The snow had hardened off a bit once he got deeper into the bush, so he didn't sink in too much, and, yeah, he was sweating, but the wind that found its way through the trees soon dried his face off.

The cold revived him. Cleared his head. By the time he'd made it up *Everest — the Return,* he came to a decision. Once he'd settled in at the camp, he was going straight up to the shack on the hill and contact his folks — come clean. He began to compose the text message. He'd offer to come back tomorrow, on the Friday train, if they wanted. He'd check with them Friday morning.

"Had to do it," he'd text. He wouldn't try to explain. They'd either get it or they wouldn't get it; either way he'd take the con-sequences. The decision bloomed in him as something right. Since the train wouldn't be back until around one or so tomorrow afternoon, he might even have time to dig out the Ski-Doo in the morning and go tool around Dead Horse Bay, have a quick look.

Or maybe he wouldn't.

He wanted so much to be the one to find Dodge, no matter how horrible it would be. It was what a best friend should do. He didn't need Dodge in his dreams demanding him to come to know that. He didn't owe Dodge anything. Not really. His dad had made sure he understood that.

"You couldn't have stopped him," Burl had said.

"Mr. Hoebeek?"

"Or Dodge."

"I could have stopped Dodge. And Trick would have listened to me."

"Yeah, well . . ."

He shook the memory out of his head. He'd go take a look, swing around the bay in the sled, and then do right by his parents.

He passed the halfway point. It was pretty well all downhill from there. He felt better already, full of optimism. His load felt lighter. Hah! A cliché, but completely true nonetheless.

He came to a tree weighed down with snow, its trunk cracked. It was tipped diagonally across the trail so that he had to duck low to get under it. Every spring his father came up early with the chain saw to clear the fallen trees from the trail. By then, this would be one of them. It was big, probably a foot thick. He patted the trunk and the nearest branch above dumped a weight of snow on his head.

"All right, already. Lesson learned," he shouted at the tree, laughing as he dug the snow out of his collar. It was good to laugh.

He knew every turn of the trail, and as he got closer and closer to the lake his sense of excitement grew, not to mention his hunger. Finally, he passed the trail that led off to his right to the Hoebeeks' camp. Two hundred yards to go. His first lunch would come before he set off back to the track. His second lunch would come upon his return. That would leave a good few hours before he cooked supper. By then the camp would be toasty warm. He had a thriller to read on his Kindle, some new music downloaded on his phone, and there were cards if he wanted to play some solitaire.

It was all good. It was all going to be okay.

And then suddenly he stopped dead. It wasn't all good.

It wasn't going to be okay at all.

# Trespass

A door opened. Just that. The scariest sound in the world.

There was one more turn in the trail before he arrived at the open ground where the camp stood, overlooking the lake. He could see the gap in the trees, up ahead. He could see a corner of the woodshed but not the camp itself, not from here. If someone crossed the yard toward the outhouse, he'd see them, though he doubted they'd see him, even if they happened to turn and look; he was on the dappled path, just another shadow. He stood perfectly still, not sure what to do. There were only two properties at the north end: the Crows' and the Hoebeeks'. After you passed the Hoebeek turnoff, the trail led directly to the Crows' and nowhere else. The trail ended at the lake.

The door he'd heard opening now slammed shut. Nate let out his breath. It wasn't his imagination. He thought it through. Something might have happened to the door. Maybe a bear had trashed it sometime last fall and it was swinging back and forth on its hinges. It was the outer door, the one into the sunporch. He doubted even a bear would have gotten through the heavy wooden door to the camp inside the porch. It had never happened before, but his father had told him tales about the damage bears could inflict. Which is why the camp had shutters on it with nails pounded into them, business side out, to douse the curiosity of any critter, animal or human. But there were no shutters on the porch door.

A door damaged by a bear: that was one possibility.

The other was that someone had just stepped out of the door and gone back inside again. By now Nate had stood stock-still for five minutes. The cold that suddenly coursed through him was only partially due to the temperature.

*Dodge.*

The idea poleaxed him.

*He survived.*

He's set himself up at the camp, living off rice and —

No, this was stupid! Impossible. It was going on four months since he'd disappeared. And it wasn't even his camp! For all Nate's fantasizing, he couldn't believe it. Calm down, he told himself. He summoned up his father: WWBD?

It's winter. What's the first thing you do when you arrive at the camp? Right: light a fire. And, to turn the old saying on its head, where there's fire, there's smoke. Why hadn't he smelled smoke? He sniffed. Nothing. So maybe the door was unhinged for some reason. He felt unhinged himself. He risked walking forward, sticking well over to the side of the path, until he reached the woodshed, where he could peek out at the camp.

Smoke.

Smoke was pouring out of the chimney, all right, but the wind was strong from the southeast, blowing the smoke across the end of the lake. He could smell it now that he was this close.

He backtracked up the trail a bit until the opening in the trees was gone from view, then he stopped and looked around, looked back the way he had come. What was going on here? He had walked in on pristine snow. No human had come in before him, not on the trail. Which meant if there was someone at the camp, they'd have had to come in from the lake.

He shrugged off the Woods pack. The physical relief was instantaneous, but there was no mental relief. He hefted the pack into the bush beside the trail.

Now what?

Better not make tracks any closer to the camp. No one in the yard would see the path he'd left unless they actually headed this way. He walked back up the trail a little farther until he found a point he could enter the bush on the eastern side. The underbrush was not too thick. As quietly as he could, Nate pushed his way through, glad of his thick winter clothing against the snagging and whipping of branches intent on snarling a person up— especially a person with serving platters on his feet. Laboriously, he made his way toward the yard but well east of the cabin, over near where the outhouse stood on its own little path at the fringe of the fenced-in garden plot. When he could see the cabin door clearly, he settled on his haunches to wait. The door was intact. There had to be someone inside.

Maybe it was some friend of his father's, someone who knew where the key was hidden. Unlikely; Burl didn't share that information widely. Occasionally he would allow some hunter or fisherman friend to stay there. He never charged anything. Didn't ever want the camp to become a rental property. Didn't much like anyone coming up here at all, except family and close friends.

Nate waited, his eyes never leaving the camp. He was breathing hard, sweating like a pig from the exertion of fighting his way through the bush. But as soon as he settled in to watch, he could feel the cold wrap its thin blue fingers around his throat. He was out of the wind but deep in the shivering shade.

His father had built the cabin from scratch. It was on the site of a camp that had burned down twenty-five years ago. His father had come to know the man who'd lived there, an eccentric musician. Burl had inherited the property from him when he was only around Nate's age. The Maestro was what Dad called him: Nathaniel Orlando Gow. Nate was named after him.

The Maestro had lived in a pyramid of glass, like nothing anyone in these parts had ever seen. Burl had built a more humble cabin out of logs on the footprint of that glass pyramid. He had taken years to do it — done it all himself, as a kind of tribute to the Maestro: harvested the trees; peeled the bark with a drawknife; built a shelter open on all four sides to dry the logs. He'd started the project when he was seventeen and had his first teaching placement before it was done. Now there was a closed-in sunporch at the front, which he'd added after marrying Astrid. When Nate was a baby, Burl had pushed out the back of the cabin to allow for two small bedrooms. But the place was still tiny: a kitchen-dining-living room in front and two bedrooms in back just big enough to stand up and turn around in, with storage areas under and over the beds, like cabins on a boat. The logs were whitewashed on the outside, with green trim around the windows and doors. It was a pretty little cabin, especially now — picturesque — the roof piled high with snow that protruded in undulating curves right out over the gutters, looking like the top of a giant mushroom. The snow was a couple feet deep except for around the chimney, where you could see the new green shingles they'd put up together two summers ago. A roofing bee — Paul and Dodge had been part of the crew. He looked at that patch of green and swallowed hard. The snow had melted, warmed by the heat in the chimney. And now that he looked closely, he could see someone had cleared the snow off the solar panels on the porch roof. Whoever was in the place had been here awhile.

Nate watched the smoke curl up into the blue, then bend under the wind.

There was a pair of snowshoes stuck in the snow by the side of the stoop, which was good and trampled down. He could see the snow riveted with yellow holes all around the entranceway. He'd peed off that stoop himself when they'd been up here in the winter, but the sight angered him now, as if some mongrel dog had been marking out his territory.

Despite a break of trees along the shore, the wind off the lake found Nate, making his eyes water. It was strong enough to raise the powder into swirling white gusts. The windbreak ended by the stairs down to the beach, right beside the cabin. The stairs were invisible now under the snow. About thirty yards out on the lake, this guy — he assumed it was a guy — had dug a hole for water. He could see the corners of a sheet of plywood with snow piled on it as insulation so that the hole didn't freeze up. Whoever he was, the man was no stranger to the bush.

And he knew where to find stuff. The ice auger was kept in the work shed off the little garage where they kept the Kawasaki. And that shed key was hidden separately from the house key. Was this a good thing, maybe? If this trespasser knew where all the keys were, he must be someone familiar with the place. Maybe this was all just some weird screwup: maybe Burl had told the guy months ago he could stay there and then forgotten about it. Nate shook his head. His dad didn't make mistakes like that. But maybe the friend had gotten the dates mixed up somehow.

*Dodge.*

Stop it, he told himself, angry now. No more denial. *He's dead — can't you get that through your thick head?*

Nate's eyes wandered out to the lake again. There were no tracks on the snow beyond the water hole. No tracks at all.

How was that possible?

There should have been snowmobile tracks, or at least snow-shoe tracks, unless the guy had been here for ages, since before the last big fall. When was that? Nate tried to think when they'd had a big snowfall in Sudbury. A couple of weeks or so ago, he thought. Maybe more.

Had this guy moved in?

Then the door of the cabin was suddenly flung open again and a man stepped out. Not Dodge. Not a boy, lean and blond, who ran cross-country, but a grown man in black jeans and a shapeless mustard-yellow sweater coming undone at the cuffs and waist. He had a colorful wool scarf wrapped around and around his neck. Nate knew that scarf, knew it was six feet long. His mother had knitted it. The man wore wraparound shades with glittery silver frames. The sides of his head were shaved, but he had a thatch of black hair and a few days' growth on his chin. He took a long draw on a can of beer. While he might have been around the same age as Nate's father, he didn't look like any friend of Burl Crow's. He stood staring toward the outhouse as if he wasn't sure he could be bothered heading there. Then Nate realized his gaze was aimed higher, toward the steep hill to the east of the camp where the path meandered up to the cabin on the cliff. Why was he look-ing there? Nate shook his head. He was just imagining it. Nobody knew about the shack. Its owner was long since dead. The cabin was a Northender secret.

By now the man on the stoop was shivering from the cold. He tipped his beer for a last swallow and then hurled the can out into the snow before he went back inside. The wind immediately caught the empty blue aluminum can and danced it across the yard toward the bush. There were other beer cans there, like a flock of small birds huddling in the underbrush.

Definitely no friend of his father's.

Which meant . . . What?

There was no going back. The Budd would have passed Bisco by now on its way northwest and wouldn't be back this way until tomorrow afternoon. There might be someone at the south end of the lake, at Sanctuary Cove. Over the years he'd met a few people from down that way, but he didn't know any of them by name apart from Likely La Cloche, and he got around on crutches these days, so it was unlikely he'd be up in March. Maybe some ice fishermen, but . . . No, the whole idea of trekking twenty kilometers into the teeth of the wind was nuts. It would be dark before he got there, with no guarantees there would be anyone to take him in.

Nate looked again at the camp. He tried to imagine knocking on the door. "Hi, my name is Nathaniel Crow and you're trespassing." He didn't think that would go down any too well.

But there was somewhere close he could go.

He swallowed hard. He was shuddering already from the cold, but the thought of going over to the Hoebeeks' made him shiver deep in his bones. But wait, there was somewhere else!

*First sign of any trouble . . .*

"Up the hill," said Nate to himself. The miner's shack. That made more sense. The path was nearby and he had been going to head up there anyway, to text his parents as soon as he could.

Might as well let them know the camp had been invaded while he was at it. His father would know what to do. Nate even began to think there might be a silver lining to this escapade. After all, he'd caught an intruder red-handed. Instead of getting a dressing down, Nate might get a medal. Yeah, right.

He pulled back into the undergrowth and set out in a wide circle around the outhouse, not wanting the man to catch sight of his snowshoe prints when he did eventually come over this way. He looked up and saw the first of the orange plastic markers, fluttering on the branch of a naked alder. But even as he veered toward the path that led to the cliff, he saw something he really didn't want to see, and it stopped him dead.

Snowshoe tracks leading up the hill in a zigzag path through the bush.

This was getting truly weird. Who was this guy who knew so much? Nate was too cold to stop and think anymore. The upside of this discovery was that he wouldn't have to break trail and he could get up there all the faster. Then he did stop and think. He thought about the guy on the stoop staring in this direction. And even as he thought about just why the intruder might have been doing that, he looked up the hill himself and saw another one of them coming down.

The sunlight slanting through the trees hit the man, mercifully too busy keeping his eye on the steep path to bother looking beyond the toes of his snowshoes. Nate shrank back into the trees and waited silently, out of sight, trying to keep his chattering teeth from giving him away. This one was meatier, dressed properly for the cold with the hood of his parka up and the string drawn tight under his chin. There wasn't a lot of face visible, but Nate could see he was frowning, deep in thought.

He was either concentrating on the path or worried about

something. Then he reached the head of the outhouse trail and, with his ski poles in one hand, untied his hood, whipped off his toque, and shook his head like a swimmer coming up from under. As Worried Man hit the yard, Nate heard the door of the cabin open a third time, as if Shades had been waiting. He crossed his arms, looked amused.

"My, my," he said. "You look like Santa didn't leave you that new bike you were hoping for."

"They can't make it," said Worried Man.

"Why am I not surprised?" Shades said, and laughed. There wasn't anything cheerful about the sound.

"There's some good news," said Worried Man. "A chance to get outa here without the bird."

"Well, well," said Shades, on an enthusiastic upnote. "Bye-bye, birdie. Is this Brother Kev's doing?"

"Yeah," said Worried Man. "He has a plan." By then, he had reached the cabin, where he ditched his poles and stood with his legs apart, his hands on his hips, his back arched, breathing hard. "We need to check back with him."

Shades nodded, took off his sunglasses, and massaged his closed eyes with a thumb and forefinger. Worried Man kicked off his snowshoes, and whatever else the two men said was lost to Nate as they reentered the camp.

Any chance of heading up to the miner's cabin was lost. If they were going back there to check with Kev, who knew how long he would have? Should he wait it out? No, he was too cold. He knew he could only make the trip if he could light a fire once he got there and get some food in him. He couldn't take that chance now. He needed shelter right away, and there was only one option left. A place he knew well. A place he loved. A place he had spent many summers in and out of. And a place he could barely imagine entering.

# Refuge

It was one thing working up some body heat tromping in from the track, knowing a warm fire and lunch were waiting. But hanging about in the shadows had dropped Nate's core temperature far too low. He needed to get warm, and soon.

As quickly as possible, he made his way back to where he'd left the Woods pack, strapped it on, and then backtracked up the trail to the fork that led to the Hoebeeks' place. He was about to turn down that trail but stopped himself just in time. There was a chance somebody would find the path he'd made coming in from the train. The last thing he needed to do was lead them right to the Hoebeeks' door. So he tromped up the trail a bit farther until he found a conveniently bushy spot and literally dove in, rolling on one shoulder and not quite making it to his feet again. Instead, his snowshoes tangled and he ended up on his back. With the Woods pack on, he felt as vulnerable as a flipped turtle. It was almost funny. He stared up at the tall trees rising above him seeming to converge as if toward a heavenly vanishing point. The tops swayed, mesmerizing. The snow wasn't cold when you were lying in it. Not really. He was this lumpy snow angel.

A vision of Art and Trick Hoebeek lying in their PFDs flashed before his eyes — their faces staring up into the November sky, their arms out to their sides, skin as white as paper, mouths too numb to speak, as the freezing water of Ghost Lake sucked the last calories of heat out from them.

Nate scrambled to his feet. He stood for a moment, regaining his balance. He hadn't been there to see them like that, but the image was fixed in his head anyway. He was dizzy from the fall, from hunger. He was losing it. And he still had a hard slog ahead of him. He glanced back out at the trail where his northbound steps stopped abruptly. There was nothing to show he'd dived into the bush, but what did he expect they'd think if they followed the trail back to this point? That he'd just flown away? Been airlifted — picked up in a UFO tractor beam? He shook his head. It was the best he could do.

It took him close to twenty minutes to fight his way through the bush to a spot directly behind the Hoebeeks' place, a distance he could have walked in three minutes on the path they'd made from his place to Dodge's, through the glade of trees that separated the two camps. Directly before him was the shed where the Hoebeeks kept their four-by-four and snowmobile. Art was one of those swaggering men who was all about Go Big or Go Home. Only the top model of anything was going to be good enough. And right now, that 600 Indy Polaris in the shed was giving Nate ideas. But that would have to wait. All he could afford to think about was getting out of the cold.

He was about to cut between the motor shed and the

woodshed to the camp, which was only about fifteen yards away across open ground, when he realized that a path directly from where he stood to the back door would be visible if one of the intruders happened to wander over this way. He leaned forward, his hands on his knees, the weight on his back oppressive. He closed his eyes. To hell with it, he thought. And then he imagined his father by his side, calm and strong. Waiting. Waiting for Nate to figure it out.

He groaned. Then, reluctantly — and with a few foul words thrown in — he made his way still farther west, circling the Hoebeeks' place, wading through the brush like a man through a swamp all the way around to the far side of the house, until finally he was in a place where his tracks would be completely out of sight. And all the time now, the smoke from his own camp was in his nose as if taunting him: a warm fire in his own woodstove and here he was only a hundred yards away playing hide-and-seek.

He knew where the Hoebeeks' key was hidden. He knew this place almost as well as his own. They had built a brand-new two-story camp about three years ago, a bigger, fancier place than the Crows', suitable for a family of five — what *had* been a family of five back then. There were only the two of them left now, Dodge's mom, Fern, and baby Hilton. Nate somehow doubted she'd ever come here again. So he was looking at a ghost house, he thought, and then immediately wished he hadn't.

He made his way around to the back door, on the north side of the camp. He stayed close to the wall, inching along, hoping the disturbed snow wouldn't stand out too much so close to the building. It didn't really matter anymore; the only thing Nate was thinking about was the woodstove in the living room. He knew for a fact there would be dry wood stacked right beside the stove in a deep box: wood and kindling and paper, matches on the shelf above. It was the way you left camp — ready for the next person who came up.

Having shucked off his snowshoes, Nate opened the door with shaking hands and closed it behind him. It was pitch-black inside. The place was completely boarded up on the main floor. As his eyes adjusted, he could see some light drifting down the staircase from the second-floor landing window. None of the windows upstairs were boarded, but the bedroom doors were closed.

He leaned his back against the door, breathing hard. It was only slightly warmer inside than out. He could do something about that, but he'd need to be able to see what he was doing. After a moment, he opened the door again to let in some light and then rummaged through the pack for his headlamp. He found it, put it on, and hauled the Woods pack inside. He closed the door again and then remembered his snowshoes. Wasn't much point in leaving no tracks if you left the damn snowshoes and poles sitting on the back stoop for all to see.

It was spooky, looking at this otherwise familiar place through a flashlight's beam.

"Dodge?"

He whispered the name. Waited. Nothing. What did he expect? He knew he was being absurd, but he had to say it. What he hadn't counted on was that talking out loud in the dark only made the whole thing eerier still. It wasn't as if he really believed Dodge was there, not the Dodge he knew anyway. But in the deep gray dimness that surrounded the cone of light from his headlamp, it wasn't hard to believe another Dodge might be lurking around here somewhere. An angry, otherworldly Dodge — a ghostly wanderer with every right in the world to demand another shot at life in whatever form he could grab it.

"Dodge, if you're here, it's me, Nate."

The wind buffeted the lake side of the house, but there were other, smaller sounds: creakings and scurryings. In his headlamp's beam, he located the mousetrap in the middle of the kitchen floor. The Hoebeeks had modeled it on the patented Burl Crow method: a bucket with a thin metal rod piercing either side near the rim. The rod held in place a pop can laced with peanut butter; a wooden plank led from the floor to the lip of the bucket. From there it was no big leap for a hungry mouse to the tasty treat spread on the pop can. Except once it made that leap, the pop can rolled on its axle and the mouse ended up in the liquid at the bottom — antifreeze, to keep the smell down. Nate looked inside. There were six small corpses. Six!

He backed away. They'd occasionally find one at his place, but six? He looked around, caught sight of a live one that stopped for a moment, caught in the spotlight, then scampered away.

He saw another and another. The place was infested. Which was very, very weird. It was a new place, and the Hoebeeks were every bit as strict about closing up as the Crows were. Then he remembered: they *hadn't* closed up. His dad had done it, on his own, after the failed search for Dodge in November. He'd have done it right but he'd have done it alone, and who knew what state his head was in. He'd been in the search party. Still, that didn't explain an explosion in the mouse population. Nate didn't want to think what did explain it, but a barrage of haunted-house images crowded his brain. He growled and shook it off. All he knew was that he wasn't going to be able to take this much darkness if an army of mice were going to be sharing the place with him.

The Hoebeeks' place was open concept but much roomier and more modern than the Crow camp, and with the benefit of a second floor. When you came in the back door, the kitchen was to your right and a bathroom was to your left, complete with a composting toilet. So — hallelujah — no need for the outhouse. Mind you, it wasn't going to flush in below-freezing temperatures. So it was really just a glorified chamber pot. Whatever — beggars can't be choosers.

There was a deep closet-type pantry to the right of the bathroom door and then the staircase to the second floor. There was a counter separating the kitchen from the dining area, and the living room was to the left, just past the stairwell. Off the living room and around the corner from the staircase, there was a door leading to the master bedroom. The stove, a big green Vermont Castings beauty, was against the east wall. The front door to their camp led out onto the Hoebeeks' expansive front deck overlooking the lake. There were picture windows to either side of the door, but they were boarded up. Everything was boarded up but for the windows upstairs. There was a skylight up there, too, he remembered, not that it made one iota of difference now, covered by snow.

There was only one window that faced west — faced away from the Crows' camp. Only one window that Shades and Worried Man couldn't see if they just happened to mosey over. It was the window above the kitchen sink. The shutters were affixed on the outside. It was painful to even think of going back out again, but better now than after he'd gotten a fire started and was beginning to thaw. With the promise of that fire to look forward to, Nate turned toward the back door and immediately lost his footing — slipped right out — and only managed to keep from falling by grabbing the kitchen counter.

He swore. He'd forgotten how slippery the laminate flooring was. But then he shouldn't have been wearing his snowy boots inside. He shook his head and tiptoed toward the door, opened it, and took in a good, deep dollop of cold air. The wind off the lake was picking up, from the sound it was making on the front wall, but he was in its lee back here, and it gave him the courage to venture out again. He didn't bother with the snowshoes, could hardly imagine summoning up the energy to bend over and strap them on. Instead, he edged his way along beside the camp, around the corner to the west wall on the hardened snow left by his earlier tracks. He got to work. There were four barrel-bolts holding the shutter in place. It was done in no time. He pulled down the three-by-five-foot plywood shutter and leaned it against the wall. No need to hide it. If they came this far, they'd know something was up. Then he raced inside, glad to see the difference the one seeing-eye window made in a blind house.

The wood was dry. The fire burned hot. Stripping down to his socks, long underwear, and a turtleneck, Nate pulled a chair up by the stove to absorb every BTU it was pumping out. For one brief moment before he lit the fire, he had thought about waiting until dark so there was no chance they'd see the smoke. It would have been a worthy precaution but not one his trembling body could accept. Besides, he rationalized, the wind seemed to have shifted and was coming in directly off the lake now; the smoke would be blown northward; chances were good it wouldn't even rise as high as the trees between the two camps.

The wind battered the building. It groaned in its mooring. Nate looked around in the growing shadows. It was going on five and the sun would soon be blocked out by the hills to the west. He was not looking forward to the night.

Just one night, he told himself.

As his brain thawed out, he formulated a plan. He'd get up early and hit the trail in plenty of time. He wouldn't bother sneaking away. He'd walk straight up the Hoebeeks' lane to the fork. They find his tracks, big deal — he'd be gone. He wasn't sure when the big storm was due to roll through, but there was little chance the train would be on time anyway, so once he got to the railroad, he'd just keep walking, heading southeast, following the tracks; the farther away, the better. He could walk on the tracks, which would be a heck of a lot easier than slogging through the snow.

In the luxury of warmth and with a full belly, he thought again about the big snowmobile out back in its shed. The Hoebeeks had come up with an ingenious system. There were doors front and back to the shed and inside a ramp leading up to a steel platform about three feet off the ground. That's where the Polaris sat. The front opening to the shed featured a Dutch door with the split at the same height as the platform, so you didn't have to clear the snow in front of the door to launch the snowmobile. There were a couple of portable ramps you could fix to the front of the platform, out over the lower door and onto the snow, however deep it was.

So. There was a fast sled out there. And as far as Nate could see, the guys next door did not have one, other than his dad's old Ski-Doo. But he'd seen no tracks to suggest they'd used it. He could get out of here fast. The thing is, he'd have to leave the Polaris out at the trailhead. If his life were in danger, doing that wouldn't be so bad. Was his life in danger? He thought about those guys back at the camp. What were they doing there? It seemed like they had complete access, but the only things worth ripping off were the Kawasaki four-by-four, which they couldn't use in deep snow, the ancient Ski-Doo, a couple of outboard motors, a generator out in the shed, and a few power tools. There was a new trapper sled for the Ski-Doo, so they could transport some stuff out if they wanted, but they sure didn't seem to be in any hurry. Thieves would have hit and moved on. These guys seemed to have moved *in*.

So what did that mean? Well, for one thing it probably meant that Nate didn't need to "escape," he just needed to get out, which meant firing up the Polaris and leaving it out at the track was basically a whole lot of wasted time. He shook his head. Couldn't deal with any of this now. He'd sleep on it.

Ah, sleep . . . How exactly was that going to happen?

He was counting on the intruders next door not seeing the smoke from the chimney, but he'd sleep upstairs anyway, just in case they did see it and came around to investigate. If he was upstairs and anyone came in, Nate would know about it, with half a chance of protecting himself. Then he wondered why exactly he was thinking this way. They were two yahoos who'd broken into his camp. Who knew what they were up to? But did he really expect trouble from them as long as he stayed out of their way?

Before it got entirely dark, he made a trip outside and around to the front corner of the cabin, the side facing the lake. He couldn't see the hole they'd made in the ice from this vantage point because the brush between the two camps stretched right down to the shore. Even if they went out there to haul up water, they wouldn't be able to spot the Hoebeeks' chimney. It didn't really matter in the end. He'd die without the stove. The weatherman had predicted twenty-five below again tonight. And as for water for himself, he'd be stuck melting snow.

As soon as he'd gotten the fire raging, he'd dug out a box of mac and cheese and poured the contents into a boiling pot of melted ice on the woodstove. He also had Tetra Paks of milk. Butter was in the cooler out at the track, but he found some cooking oil in the pantry; it had frozen solid and looked pretty disgusting, but he wasn't about to wait around for it to melt. The Ziploc bags of good stuff — baked beans, stew, and chili — were a very long hike away, along with the meat, cheese, and eggs. So mac and cheese it was. And toast made from bread pretty badly squashed from when he'd turtled out. The Hoebeeks had electricity run by a generator, which, obviously, he wasn't about to turn on. Luckily, they still had an old-fashioned toaster, just like the Crows, basically a square of perforated tin with four wire frames sticking up at an angle on the top, against which you could rest the bread. He put four slices on to toast, turning them so that they burned equally on both sides.

As the darkness set in, he decided that sleeping upstairs was probably not a good plan. He'd be feeding the fire all night. Better just to stay put. He manhandled the queen-size mattress from the downstairs bedroom and tugged it right up close to the stove. There was a big trunk on the landing upstairs where the family kept bedclothes. He gathered blankets and pillows and curled up in the warm. It was early, not yet eight, but he was exhausted and aching all over. The day had started with a lie to the man he most admired in the whole world. It had gone downhill from there. And now he was lying in the house of a dead friend, more alone than he could have ever imagined it was possible to be. And sleep . . . sleep was going to be an almighty struggle. It was a precious cargo shackled to a sinking ship of worries.

# Dodge's Return

In horror movies, there was always a lot of rodent activity when there were ghosts around. But it wasn't mice that were thumping around outside on the front deck. And the voices were not the voices of mice.

"For God's sake, Trick, hold up your end!"

"Give me a break. I'm trying."

"Boys, that's enough bellyaching."

"Ow!" Trick howled. "Dad, Dodge kicked me."

"Did not."

"Did, too."

"Boys, I'm warning you!" There was an exaggerated sigh. "I swear, sometimes . . ." said Art Hoebeek, but he didn't continue, and Nate was left to wonder what it was he swore.

The front doorknob rattled. It rattled again.

"Who locked the door? Dodge?"

"No way, Dad. How could I?"

Art swore under his breath while the boys shoved each other around and quibbled. Then there was the unmistakable sound of a key fitting into a lock, and the front door swung open.

"Okay, fellas, let's get this done."

Before Nate's eyes, three moonlit figures entered the camp from the front deck, carrying between them a gleaming white Servel propane refrigerator. Big Art out front and the boys each at a corner of the end, Trick's corner drooping, Dodge scoffing, their father growling. They passed right by Nate sitting up on his mattress by the fire. Didn't seem to see him at all. He tore his eyes away from the grim parade heading toward the kitchen and stared out the open door. The snow was gone, the lake shimmered with luminescence, and the water lapped gently against the beach. The silvery sides of a sixteen-foot aluminum boat pulled up on the shore glittered in the moonlight.

Nate stared toward the kitchen, where the trio had deposited the fridge. They were standing there not doing anything, their backs to him. Then they turned, one by one: Art and then Trick and Dodge last of all. They were soaking wet, their clothes hanging from them in tatters and their skin so white it glowed as brightly as the refrigerator. Their eyes were hollow, their expressions numb. They stood there like statues. Then slowly, Dodge separated himself from the others and walked like a zombie toward Nate until he stood above him, dripping cold water on his bedclothes, his face.

"This is on you, man." A hand that was mostly bone pointed back toward the kitchen, to his father. "You could have stopped him, Numbster. Why didn't you come?"

Nate lay in his bed wide awake, grabbing at breath hungrily, as if he'd just run a marathon. He glanced at the front door. Closed.

Shuttered. He listened to the sounds of the night, the wind banging about as if some giant were pressing his massive shoulder to the southern wall, determined to push the camp back into the forest.

A mouse ran across the foot of his bed. He slapped the floor beside the mattress with the flat of his hand, heard the skittering. Meanwhile he tried to rein in his breathing, talk himself down. Tomorrow was going to be crazy, and he would need every ounce of energy he could muster.

It's just a dream, he told himself. But he thought of how Dodge always finished what he started, no matter what. He'd set out with his father and little brother on a mission. It was hard not to believe they wouldn't be here any moment.

He slammed his hand down on the floor again.

Sleep, he told himself. Or if not sleep, rest. He thought about his parents, imagined his mother doing homework at the dining room table and his father sitting in the living room nearby, reading — neither of them with any idea of the predicament he was in. He thought about Shades and Worried Man and wondered what they were up to over in the Crow camp. Anger made his stomach grip. *That* was where he should be! Where he knew his way around. A ghost-free zone. He didn't mind being alone, *there*.

"Dodge?"

"Right. Dodge Hoebeek," he says. He's eight, like Nate, but three months older and light years cooler in his gold-and-navy-blue Pacers shorts. They're meeting for the first time down on the shore, where the new boy is skipping stones on the placid water. He lets a rock fly. Gets five skips out of it.

Nate kicks around the sand a bit, trying to think of something else to say, somewhat in awe of this boy with really long blond hair and actual biceps. He bends down and picks up a flat but jagged-edged piece of slate. "Look at this," he says.

"You can't skip that," says Dodge. "It'd never go anywhere."

"I know," says Nate, "it's an arrowhead."

Dodge takes it from him. "Really? It doesn't look like one."

"Well, not exactly. It's what's left over when you make an arrowhead."

"Yeah, right."

"It's true. There was this archeologist here and she said it. They're all over the place."

So they look for them and Dodge finds one. "There's lots of them," he says, as if it's true now that he's proven it to be so. He grins and his eyebrows float upward, as if shards of prehistoric arrow make just about anything possible.


Dodge. A lonely figure in the dark, his clothes tattered, his blond hair all woven about with the plant life that only grows in the darkest reaches of the lake, holding out a hand, so white it glowed, in supplication.

*Why didn't you come?*

# The Seeker

Nate checked his cell phone: 9:14 p.m.

He sat up, put on his headlamp, and climbed to his stocking feet. He shivered and fed the woodstove. Then he stood at the bottom of the stairs, looking up into the deeper darkness, where there was no glow from the fire to lend it any warmth. It had been one thing to venture up to the landing for blankets; had he ever really thought he could sleep up there — sleep in Dodge's old room? Then again, could he imagine actually trying to sleep without having a look around? Not now. He was wide awake and possessed.

There was Dodge's mitt on the chest of drawers across from the bunk beds. The old scuffed hardball still sat in the pocket, yellowed with age. Dodge had told him he'd caught it at a Cubs game — a loud foul ball by Ramírez, back in 2010. Nate had never cared much whether it was true or not. With Dodge, you took everything with a pinch of salt. Beside the mitt was the

V303 Seeker, sleek and white. Nate picked up the drone. The GoPro video cam was still mounted in the frame on the bottom. He sat on the edge of the lower bunk, the copter in his hands. Dodge had bought it only last spring, brought it up with him for the summer. They'd taken it to the jumping rock on the eastern flank of Picnic Island and taken turns filming each other aerially. There was one piece of footage where Dodge had brought the drone in so close over Nate's head, he could almost grab it out of the air as he plummeted toward the lake.

One day they'd taken the Seeker out in the boat and flown it up high over the eagle's nest on the tallest tree on Garbage Island to see if there were any eggs. They made the mistake of telling Burl, who put a kibosh on any further attempts. "You don't want to scramble those eggs, boys," he'd said.

They'd flown the quadcopter out to hover over Art Hoebeek when he was fishing until he stood up in the boat and shook his fist at the thing. He was yelling; Nate could see that through his binoculars. Luckily, he was too far out for Nate to hear what he was saying.

"The darn thing's worse than a squadron of mosquitoes," Mr. H. said when he returned to shore. "Scared the damned fish away."

"C'mon, Dad. It's no noisier than a power drill."

"More like a leaf blower," his father argued. "And anyway, I didn't drive seven hundred miles to have a power tool hovering over my head."

"How many kilometers would that be, Dad?"

Dodge loved to tease his father, mostly because it didn't take much. He was a man with a good enough sense of humor and a laugh as big as he was, but with a low tolerance for pranks.

Nate clutched the quadcopter more tightly. Too bad Mr. H. hadn't had a lower tolerance for tragic and idiotic stunts.

Nate swallowed hard, grabbing hold of a good memory: he and Dodge on the beach, operating the Seeker, taking it higher and higher up into the August sky until there was no sound from it at all.

"Hey, the green light came on," says Nate. His neck is craned, watching through his binoculars. Dodge is at the controls. It's the first time Nate's seen the thing fly. Dodge smiles, his eyes fixed on the flight of the drone.

"Contact," he says. "We've got a GPS signal. Now watch this." And with that he flips a toggle on the right shoulder of the transmitter.

"What's RTH?" says Nate.

"Return to home."

And just like that the copter returns, all by itself. Lands on the sand six feet away.

Nate put the drone back on the chest of drawers. He picked up the transmitter with its twin throttles. He held it in his hands, pulled both the throttles down at the same time to power up, and was shocked — amazed — when the four rotor blades started turning. He let go of the throttles. Caught his breath. Let the silence close in on him again. A silence filled with the skittering of mice and the bad mood of the wind.

The RTH toggle: you pushed that and the Seeker flew right back to where it started without the pilot doing anything at all. You just stood and watched. It would land as close as could be and then turn off its motor, just like that.

Return to home. "You hear that, Dodge Hoebeek?" he muttered. But there had never been such a toggle on Dodge.

Nate wished he had one himself right now.

He put down the transmitter, looked around, the LED light on his head picking out features of a room he knew every bit as well as his own tiny room over at the Crow camp. The bunk bed was for a visitor — himself more often than not. He'd be over there late, get up to go, and Dodge would say "Stay." And he'd say "I'm not your dog," and Dodge would say "Woof" and pant a bit until Nate laughed. Then he'd say "Stay" again, and, of course, he'd stay. And they'd talk until Fern came to the door. "Save it 'til the morning, boys," she'd whisper. Then when she'd gone back downstairs, they'd talk some more but in whispers until one or the other fell asleep.

"I don't like being alone," Dodge said to him. Only once. Nate remembered thinking how much it would have taken him to say that — to show the slightest sign of vulnerability.

"I'm here," he'd said back to the invisible figure in the bunk above. Then he'd waited for Dodge to say something more, but all he heard was the steady breathing of sleep.

"I'm here," he whispered again.

There was nothing much special about the room — no posters, only a handful of paperbacks and a stack of comics. When they were at Ghost Lake, they spent as little time as possible indoors. They were out fishing or jumping off cliff faces or bodysurfing down at Ginger Ale — the name they'd given the rapids over by the dam. They'd make stuff in the workshop over at Nate's camp or sail or swim. Even when it rained, they were as likely to be outside as in.

They.

It was hard to believe there was no more "they."

There would never be another "us," another "we," as in "We're going up to the miner's cabin," or "We're going to find our way to Spider; if we're not back by nightfall, call search and rescue," or "We were wondering whether we could take the boat down to Sanctuary Cove to do some serious girl watching . . ."

He remembered flying the Seeker from a canoe on mysterious Spider Lake, the drone hovering between high walls of stone, looking for petroglyphs.

Nate fought down the raw feeling in his throat. He should never have come up here. Up to this room. Up to Ghost Lake. Not alone anyway.

He stood, looked at the empty top bunk, patted the mattress. I'm here, he thought, but there was no point to it if Dodge wasn't. He left the room, closed the door behind him softly. He stood at the top of the stairs and turned off his headlamp. Let the darkness settle, with all its creaks and mouse wanderings and low moans. Then he made his way in the dark down to the first floor, guided only by the small starlight drifting in the one exposed window over the sink. Leaning over the sink, he looked up into the night. Might be northern lights out there when it was this crystal clear. But the two camps were backed up against the hill. The only way you'd see the aurora borealis would be to go out onto the lake. He'd seen them a few times dancing on the ridge of the hills. He wasn't going to risk it tonight. He was drained. Besides, he couldn't take the chance of leaving any tracks out there. He felt kind of like a ghost himself.

He stoked the fire and lay his aching body down, pulled the scratchy blankets up around him. The sooner he slept, the sooner morning would come and he could get the hell out of here. He wrestled the headlamp off his head and lay there in the busy darkness. Then there was a metallic scraping sound. He grabbed the headlamp and switched it on. The pop can on the mousetrap was twirling but empty.

The dream again: Dodge under the ice, writhing in the black void. And then suddenly it morphed into Dodge at the window, scrabbling against the glass, making it chatter in its frame. His eyes full of moonlight, his mouth gaping but no sound coming out.

Nate sat up, disoriented, his heart pounding, his breath ragged. He focused on the rectangle of lesser darkness beyond the counter, across the room, the only window in this mausoleum. There was no face there. Just a memory. He lay back down again. Beside him the stove ticked. It would need feeding soon. It was voracious. The night was voracious, threatening to eat him up. This place wasn't really insulated for winter, and he was not insulated against this invasion of memories. He concentrated on getting his breathing back to normal again. He listened. There was something different. The wind. The wind had stopped. Nate's heart was racing, but the night at least was still.

And that brought to memory another night, well after midnight. Dodge standing outside Nate's open window over at the Crow camp, his eyes full of moonlight and mischief.

"What?"

"Down to the beach. Now!"

Nate's parents' bedroom is right next door, through walls as thin as paper. But gazing into their room as he tiptoes past, he can see they are sound asleep.

Dodge is waiting on the sand. He has the quadcopter with him. "Night flight," he says.

Oh, the Seeker soars! Up and up and out over the moonbright lake. Dodge makes it pitch and roll, do a 360, filming the whole time.

"We have ourselves a satellite," he says. In the summer darkness, it's easier to see the light on the drone's belly turn from red to green. And with GPS in place, Dodge can take his fingers off the controls. They watch the drone hover, staying in one place in the sweet summer air, their own small star. Hovering, waiting for its next command.

"You're leaving it here?"

Dodge is packing up. He turns and looks at Nate, holding the drone. He shrugs. "Back home there are all these regulations. FAA."

"What's that?"

"Federal Aviation Administration. You can't go higher than four hundred feet, blah, blah, blah. Here, the sky's the limit."

"Yeah, but—"

"*And,*" Dodge interrupts, "Dad says if I want to fly it, I have to join an airplane club."

"Oh."

"I know. A bunch of drone geeks."

"Isn't that what we are?" Nate asks him.

"*And* take classes," says Dodge, ignoring Nate's remark. "Can you imagine: drone classes?"

"That sucks."

Dodge pats the drone on its bald white head. "I'll leave it here until close-up, anyway. Maybe I'll take it back with me then."

Meaning Canadian Thanksgiving in October. "Cool," says Nate. "We can strap a turkey leg on it and deliver it to the eagles — so they can have a little Thanksgiving celebration up in their nest."

Dodge shakes his head, exasperated. "Wrong! Those are American eagles, stupid."

"So?"

"So *their* Thanksgiving isn't until November."

The memories came to Nate sharp and clear, tumbling one over the other, unsettling him and then suddenly unsettling him even more — unsettling him with an idea that made his heart start pounding hard.

He didn't stir. He made himself lie there, thinking it through. It was insane. *He* was insane. But it might work; it could. He could feel the cold gathering force again. He'd have to get up and feed the fire. And if he had to get up anyway . . .

# Night Flight

He fed the fire. And then he made his way upstairs to Dodge's narrow bedroom and gathered up the drone and the transmitter.

Could he do this?

He set the drone on the dining room table. He turned it over and released the GoPro video camera from its bay. He went and found his cell phone by the mattress and compared the weight of it, one in each hand; the cell was heavier than the camera, but not by too much.

The camera was small, but thicker in profile than his Samsung. The cell phone could slip into the mount okay, but it wouldn't stay there. But then that's what rubber bands were for. In the kitchen, he found the right drawer. The Hoebeeks had a collection of rubber bands the size of a hardball. He liberated four sturdy ones and set about seeing if he could make this work. When he was satisfied that it could, he composed the text he would send.

2 men in the camp. I'm hiding at the Hs. I'll catch the Budd
tomorrow. They don't know I'm here. They look like criminals.

The last sentence only came to him as he typed it, and with it came a shock of delayed recognition: two men hanging from a thick, knotted rope — hanging on for dear life — as a helicopter rose above the roofline of the Sudbury Jail.

"Holy shit!"

Why had it taken him so long to realize it?

In the video, they had been dressed in prison uniforms; the footage was grainy and in black-and-white, and most of the time he only saw them from the back, except for occasionally when the rope twisted. He wasn't sure how he knew, but he was sure of it. How else could they have gotten to the camp without coming in on the trail or from the lake? They must have arrived by helicopter.

Oh.

. . . a chance to get outa here without the bird.

Of course. Wasn't that what Worried Man had said? And wasn't that another word for a chopper, a whirlybird? It all made some kind of terrible sense. And yet it made no sense at all. A dire kind of coincidence. More like a paranoid's dream come true. This is what happens when you lie to your parents: the last terrible thing you saw on the news *happens to you*.

Why here? And where was the bird — the helicopter?

It was no use trying to figure it out. He changed what he had typed:

Escapees from Sudbury Jail have taken the camp! I'm hiding
in the Hs. I'll catch the Budd tomorrow. They don't know I'm
here.

He pushed send and the message appeared in its bubble. He watched, hoping beyond hope that the word "delivered" would appear under the text, but there was no way, not down here. He knew that. He didn't even have one bar of service. But maybe he could get some bars without heading up the cliff.

He just needed elevation.

He attached the cell phone to the belly of the quadcopter. Shook the drone to see if the phone moved. No, it was nice and snug. Then he checked again to make sure the payload was dead center — balanced. It looked good. Felt secure.

He'd left his outerwear draped over dining room chairs set all around the fire. It was warm to put on and he was glad of it. He'd do without his mitts, he thought. They would be too unwieldy while operating the controls. Then he imagined his father standing nearby, not saying anything. Just waiting for Nate to figure it out.

Right.

At this kind of temperature, exposed skin would be frostbitten in about ten minutes, max. He had brought a pair of gloves as well, in case he had to do anything outside requiring dexterity. They weren't as warm as his mitts, but they'd do. He didn't plan on spending any more time out there than he had to. He picked up the transmitter, jiggled the throttles. He could operate it with the gloves. Or maybe he could get everything set up and then quickly take them off if he needed to.

He got to the door, opened it, and stepped out into a night as still as glass. He would wear his snowshoes. Had to. He needed to get away from the cabin and the trees — down to the beach or maybe even a little way out onto the lake. No, he couldn't risk that, unless he stuck real close to the underbrush and walked west along the shore a bit. And anyway, even if they did see his tracks, it wouldn't matter because he wasn't going to wait until noon to leave. He'd be gone as soon as he could if all went well.

As he passed under the kitchen window, he saw the black plywood shutter leaning against the house. Perfect! He'd need that. He balanced the quadcopter in one hand, picked up the shutter, and, stowing it under his arm, hefted it to the beach. He found a flat place and laid the shutter down, made it as horizontal as he could on the snow. This would be his launch site. The drone wasn't that heavy, but it would sink in the snow, which wasn't going to help with liftoff.

The stillness was eerie. There was a weather warning. This was the calm before the storm. So be it. Luck was on his side, finally. There's no way he could have launched the drone into the wind that had assaulted the cabin earlier. The downside was that there was nothing to drown out the sound of the drone taking off. He held the contraption over his head and pushed the cell phone's home button. It was 11:35. Would the guys next door still be up? He peered toward the Crow camp. He couldn't see it from here, but he figured he would be able to see something if there were lights on over there. Nothing.

*I'm hiding in the Hs.*

That was the message. Not *"we're* hiding." It didn't matter. No need for lying anymore. He called up the text and pressed send again.

Then he placed the drone on the landing pad, took off his gloves, and shoved them in his parka pockets. He powered up. The four propellers started whirring. Now lift. There was a hesitation, but then — sure enough — slow but steady, the craft took off from the plywood launchpad and began to climb into the dark sky. The red lights were blinking, but he hadn't expected anything less. The thing was to get it high enough. Come to think of it, he had no idea whether finding the satellite that allowed for GPS control would mean he could send the text message, but it was worth a try. Worth freezing for a few minutes.

The rise was slow, the noise irritating but not too loud. Just in case, he throttled the chopper out toward the lake and westward, the farther from the Crow camp, the better. Up, up it went, higher into the night, wobbling a bit as it found a stray breeze up there, something trickling in over the northern hills, he guessed, because the drone seemed to want to head south down the lake.

"Steady on," he heard Dodge's voice in his head. "Easy, Nate. God, she's beautiful!"

And then he saw what he'd been hoping for: the lights turned green.

"Houston, we have contact!" It was Dodge's voice in his head.

He operated the left throttle to make the Seeker do a slow 360. He hadn't the foggiest idea how cellular technology worked, but he was going to give this thing every fricking chance he could. Higher it rose, and higher. Then he pulled both of his thumbs from the spring-action throttles to let the drone just hover. Maybe his mother would still be up, would receive the text right now and answer him. His hands were already tingling — hot, with the cold. He couldn't exactly imagine standing out here long enough to send her another text, but it would be amazing — so incredibly comforting — to know he'd gotten through.

The Seeker hovered, just as it was supposed to do, but only for a moment, and then it started to keel toward the south, pushed by some unseen force. There was some kind of turbulence up there — something Nate couldn't feel down here. The front moving in from the north, he guessed, rising up over the hill and swooping down into the basin of the lake while he stood in its lee. He tried to regain manual control but the copter was fighting him.

Desperate now, he turned to the RTH toggle on the right shoulder of the transmitter.

"Turn back," he whispered to the drone. "Return to home."

It was supposed to do this all by itself, but he could see the green light had turned red again. He had lost his GPS lock. Which meant manual operation was all he had, except he was shaking now and the machine didn't seem to want to do his bidding anyway.

Dodge was the master of this craft; where was he when you fricking needed him?

Nate groaned. He had lost all feeling in his hands; he was shaking every bit as much as the copter, but now was no time to put on his gloves. Desperately he played the throttles, but the drone was out of his control, spinning, pitching, and rolling — sashaying about like it didn't know whether it was coming or going. And then suddenly, for no reason he could grasp, the Seeker plummeted, like a duck hit by a shotgun blast.

It was all over in a matter of seconds. The drone hit the lake and burrowed into the snow. For an instant, he could see a blurry red light from under the surface, and then it went out.

Shivering, Nate dropped the transmitter on the plywood launchpad and grabbed his gloves. He pulled them on and then his mitts over them and then shoved his hands into his armpits, staring out at the lake where the crash had taken place. It was over toward the enemy camp, maybe twenty yards out from the water hole, as far as he could guess, for there was nothing but starlight to go by now. And there was no way he could go over there to retrieve it. They'd see his tracks right off, the minute they looked out the sunporch window, which was the first thing anybody ever did at camp when they got up.

"Looking to see the lake's still there," Astrid liked to say.

Well, it was there, all right, even if it was buried under snow and ice so thick you could drive a truck across it.

Return to home.

Go. Back. Inside.

There was nothing else he could do. He had either sent out an SOS or not. But it was no use calling for help if you ended up freezing to death doing it. He grabbed the transmitter and shoved it in his jacket pocket. He picked up the plywood panel, no longer anything so special as a launchpad. He trudged back toward the H-camp.

It's all good, he told himself, shaking with the cold. That's what Dodge said all the time, even if it wasn't — even if they were in trouble over one of his crazy schemes. "It's all good, buddy."

Well, what could he do? If the message didn't go through, then nothing had changed, really, other than that he'd lost his not-fully-paid-for cell phone and a three-hundred-dollar quadcopter all at the same time. He'd get out of here tomorrow. That was still the goal. By this time tomorrow night, he'd be sleeping in his own bed. All he had to do was hang tight. Nothing was going to go wrong. Nothing else.

# The Masked Stranger

He could hear the drone in his dream. Or was it a dream? In his vaguely conscious mind, he imagined the Seeker had somehow come back to life, its four rotors desperately trying to drag the copter and its electronic cargo up, up, up out of the grip of the snow. The sound grew louder and louder, as if it had made it — was even now floating up into the air! Closer still! The noise rattling the air above his head as if it had somehow found its way right into the camp, until at last Nate was awake enough to realize it was not a drone but something much bigger. A chain saw? No. A rescue plane? No. Something drawing near.

A snowmobile.

He scrambled out of his tangle of covers. He raced in his socks to the kitchen window, slipping on the laminate floor, his feet going out from under him and hitting the mousetrap, which sloshed. He got up again: seven dead mice.

At the window, he couldn't see a thing. He hauled himself up onto the counter and opened the window, only to be blasted by the cold, as solid as a slap across the face. He thrust his head outside, blinking furiously in the bright reflection of the sun off the snow, and craned his head toward the lake. It was no use; he couldn't see enough of it from here. Couldn't see the narrows. Anything coming this way from the south had to pass through the bottleneck of the narrows.

He threw on his boots, and in only his long underwear and turtleneck he stepped out the back door into the deep freeze. He cocked his head, listening. The noise was coming down the trail.

He hustled back into the cabin and closed the door. For one shaky, optimistic moment he wondered if it was his father. He couldn't have come by train, but there were logging roads and other trails that he'd never been on but his father probably knew about. His father had known these woods all his life; if anyone knew how to get here in an emergency, it would be Burl.

The message had gotten through. It had to be that!

If it was his father, and if that meant he had gotten the text, he would come directly to the Hoebeeks'. Nate listened and then dropped his head in dismay. The snowmobile had already passed the turnoff. And moments later he heard it come to a stop at the other camp. Would his father do that? Challenge the intruders? No. Which meant that somebody who didn't know better had arrived. Or somebody who knew perfectly well who was there.

Which is when Nate went cold all over. The newcomer knew something Shades and Worried Man didn't know: a lone traveler on snowshoes had made his way in from the tracks to the north end of Ghost Lake and then disappeared.

*Get dressed.*

After the drone incident, he'd again laid out his clothes on chairs around the fire, just like he had earlier last evening. They were warm, even though the cabin was rapidly losing heat. There was no time to mess with a fire right now. Was it worth trying to get the shutter up over the kitchen window and pretend there was no one here? No. If they came this far, they'd see the stoop. There was no way he could disguise all the coming and going betrayed by the little porch.

So?

He dressed. Clear this place up? Forget it. Hide. Now. Upstairs. Even better, there was an attic. It was reached through a trapdoor right above the top bunk in Dodge's room. He collected his wallet and Swiss Army knife on a bureau in the living room; there was pocket change on the table and the Seeker's transmitter on the counter in the kitchen. And there was a pot with congealed macaroni in it in the sink, the woodstove still hot to the touch even as the air grew colder with every moment. His presence here was everywhere.

And then there was a knock on the door.

He stood stock-still.

A louder knock. He thought of the two men he'd seen. He glanced at his pocketknife. Forget it. He raced silently to the kitchen, opened the utensil drawer, saw Dodge's filleting knife in its sheath with DH engraved badly in the leather. He drew the knife out of the sheath and —

"Kid?" The voice was low. "I'm guessin' you're nothin' but a kid."

Guessing?

"These are, what . . . twenty-five-inch Bigfoots out here?"

*His snowshoes.*

"Now, they'll take somewhere 'round a hun'red ten, hun'red fifty pounds. Somethin' like that. So maybe you're a woman."

*How could he have left his shoes outside?*

*Bang!*

The hand that smashed the door made Nate jump. Did he cry out? Maybe.

"Stop bein' a damn fool and open up. You really don't want me to huff and puff."

The voice sounded tired. Old and tired. A voice pitted and ragged from years of cigarette smoke, by the sound of it.

Nate held the knife at stomach level. He and Dodge had filleted a lot of fish in their day. Could he use it on a human?

*Bang!*

And the door flew open, smacking hard against the closed door of the bathroom.

A man stood there, silhouetted in the wintery light, his body clothed from head to foot in snowmobile gear — black boots, black bib and turtleneck, an open black parka — his face covered with a black ski mask. There was yellow piping on the ski mask around the mouth, nose, and eye openings. He looked like the villain from some Marvel comic. Snow Fiend. His hands were bare and looked as if they'd been fashioned out of wood. They were knotty and gnarled with age. It wasn't either of the guys Nate had seen yesterday. Under all the quilted garb he was probably wiry but no less frightening.

He took a step into the house and Nate backed up. The stranger faced him, less than three paces separating them. He reached for his ski mask, as if he were going to take it off, and then suddenly dropped his arm to his side. His body tensed as if whatever he'd been expecting wasn't this.

"What are you doin' here?" he said.

There was something in his voice — surprise?

Nate said nothing.

"Hah!" the masked man said, and shook his head. Then he looked hard at Nate again. "A filletin' knife, eh? Good choice. Now be a good boy and put 'er down."

Nate responded by darting it out toward the man, trying hard not to make his hand shake as he did. The man didn't so much as flinch. He turned and leisurely closed the door behind him. Then he leaned his back against it, crossing his arms. "I'll give you a count of five to put that thing down. Di'n't your daddy teach ya nothin'?"

Nate lowered the knife a little but wasn't ready to give it up. "What do you want?" he managed to say.

"I'll ask the questions, boy. And it'll go a lot better for you if I don't have to break your arm first." He chuckled grimly. "I always find it's hard for a person to answer questions any good when they're writhin' on the floor."

Nate put the knife down on the counter.

"Smart lad," said the stranger. "Now, tell me what you're doin' here."

"This is my camp," said Nate.

"Is that so?"

"Yeah. Art Hoebeek's my dad. I'm Dodge."

The man stared at him. His eyes, what Nate could see of them, were as dark as his mask. Then he nodded slowly and looked around. "Long way to come in the middle of winter . . . Dodge. . . . Was that what you called yourself?"

Nate swallowed. "We . . . we always come up at March break."

"We?"

"My friends and I."

The man made a big deal of looking around. He knocked on the bathroom door. "Anyone in there?" he said. Then he walked toward the staircase and glanced up into the gloom. "Yoo-hoo. Anybody home?" He turned back and eyed Nate.

"I got here early," said Nate.

"Ah, that's it. So they're . . . what . . . comin' in on the Budd?"

"No," said Nate, thinking quickly. "They're flying in. From Lauzon, up on 144. They should be here anytime now. Soon."

The man took two steps toward him and Nate backed up until he was leaning against the sink.

The stranger looked around the place, taking it all in. "You got a radiophone here, Dodge Hoebeek?"

"No, sir."

"Are you tellin' the truth?"

"Yes, sir."

"Good. It's about time."

"Listen, I don't know what this is all about," said Nate. "And I don't care. My friends and I, we're just up until Sunday and then we're out of here."

"Is that so?"

"They're coming —"

"Today — Friday — and heading back Sunday. Not much of a holiday, if you ask me."

"They're flying —"

"Nobody's flyin' in!" said the man, gruff and impatient suddenly. "You got that?" Nate nodded. Again, the hidden face examined him. "There's a huge damned weather front movin' in from the northwest. It dumped somethin' like two feet on Hearst. It's clobberin' Timmins as we speak, and we're next. No one's flyin' anywhere today. You got that?"

Nate nodded.

The man walked to the front room, took one of the dining room chairs, and brought it back, trapping Nate in the kitchen. He straddled the chair, resting one arm along the back of it, his eyes on full blast. He stood again and peered over the mousetrap.

"Looks like you caught yourself some dinner," he said. Maybe he smiled. It was hard to tell, but it didn't last. "This weather has screwed up our plans, too — my friends and me. Big time. But we're all just gonna have to ride it out. You got that?"

Nate nodded.

"So, here's what's gonna happen," said Masked Man. "You're gonna find a coupla buckets and get yourself some water from the hole out there on the ice. You know what I'm talkin' 'bout?" Again, Nate nodded. "Don't go anywhere near the other cabin, you hear me? Don't come lookin' for a cup of sugar or nothin' neighborly like that. Those lads are not happy about you being here, a fact they only just learnt." He snickered. "Not all that observant," he said, shaking his head. "They're not all that happy about bein' here themselves. Believe me, they'd just as soon shoot you and leave your carcass out in the bush for the wolves. Do not give them any excuse to do it. You got that?" Nate nodded a third time. "Anyway, get your water. Then get yourself a good big load of firewood — enough to get you through a coupla days — maybe more dependin' on how big this storm is."

Nate nodded solemnly.

"I'm gonna assume you've got food to get you through until Sunday, like you said, unless that was also a lie." Nate shook his head. "You don't got food?"

Nate nodded. "No. I mean, yeah. I've got some."

The man looked around. Saw the folding doors beside the bathroom. Got up from his chair and marched over. He opened the door to shelves of dry goods. "Well, lookee here," he said. Then he closed the doors and turned to face Nate. "You ain't gonna starve."

Nate nodded yet again, and the man suddenly rushed him and grabbed a mitt full of his turtleneck in his fist. "For God's sake, boy, don't stand there bobbing your head like some dash-board Jesus."

Nate's jaw locked tight. His fists curled.

The man let go of him and stepped back, one, then two paces. He made to lunge toward Nate again. This time, Nate stood his ground.

"That's more like it. Show a little gumption, for God's sake. I hate a pussy."

The man clumped toward the door. He had a slight limp. He turned, with his hand on the doorknob. "I'd advise you to get a move on," he said. "Those yahoos over there are simmerin'; you don't want them to come to a boil." He paused as if he were wait-ing for Nate to nod. Nate held his head perfectly still. The masked man seemed to smile. Nate saw a flash of gold tooth. "Once ya done all of that, lock this door and stay put. Ya hear me?"

"I hear you."

"Good." He opened the door and then turned once more, with the snow blowing in around him. He gazed at Nate for a good long time while thick flakes whirled into the room. "You don't look all that bad," he said, "for a kid who went missin' last fall and is presumed dead." Then he closed the door quietly after himself.

# 13

## Prisoner

He got the water first. There were two green plastic buckets, big ones, under the sink, so he filled them at the water hole only three-quarters full. There was an old tin dipper attached by a length of yellow rope to a spike set in the ice. Nate splashed himself a fair bit, he was so nervous, feeling the eyes of the criminals up in the camp as cold as the wind on his back. In seconds, the freezing water had soaked through his socks, the cuffs of his sweater, sneaking out from under his jacket. He moved the three-quarter-filled buckets out of the way and hauled the plywood back over the hole. He stood up, not daring to face the Crow camp, but as he picked up the buckets to head back to the Hoebeeks', he noticed something odd. Just beyond the hole was a giant circular pattern in the snow, with the ghostly remains of snowshoe tracks leading away from it toward the shore. It was like a shallow crater, maybe seven or eight yards across, as if someone had started to make a small skating rink but had given up. There was a kind of ridge around the perimeter, like a frozen wave.

He shook his head and started back toward the camp. He carried one bucket in each hand for balance. The extra weight made slogging through the snow harder. As the stranger had noted, his snowshoes weren't rated for much more weight than himself. He didn't dare to even look up in case the men were there. But he did dare to look out toward where he figured the drone had crashed last night. By now the wind swooping down over the hill was playing havoc with the snow, and there was no sign of the Seeker or its expensive cargo.

He got the wood. There was a toboggan in the woodshed and he loaded it up, but by then his mind was elsewhere, thinking about a whole other kind of sled. The one in the locked shed: the Polaris. Nate's father prided himself on keeping his eighties vintage 'Doo in good shape. It worked just fine, managed to put out around fifty-five horsepower. But Dodge could literally ride circles around Nate when they were out on the flat of the lake. He was good about sharing his toys; Nate knew how to operate the Polaris. He also knew where the keys were.

As he unloaded the first pile of firewood inside the cabin and went back for another load, he developed a plan. He'd have to work fast, but it was only about ten o'clock now. He'd wait until it was just about time for the Budd to arrive at Mile 39, with the full knowledge that it would probably be late. How late could be critical. If it was really late, he might have to take evasive actions. He was definitely not going to hang around at the trailhead now that there was a pursuit vehicle parked next door.

He'd have to book it out of camp, knowing that ski-mask guy would give chase, but Nate's brain was churning now. He remembered the tree that was already half down across the trail. He'd take an ax with him. If he got a good enough jump on the guy, he'd have time to chop the tree down behind him. There wasn't much trunk left. It would only take a swing or two.

The tree was ready to go in a strong wind — it might be down already. That would be disastrous: to get halfway up the trail and then have to veer off into the bush. Not good. The bush was too thick most places.

It was a half-assed idea, but the desire to get out of there was strong. He decided to just pray the tree was still standing and ready to fall — with him on the other side of the trail. It would give him some time. It could work. Whatever the man said about the coming storm, the Budd would get there eventually.

"It's a quarter-assed plan," said Dodge in his head. "Maybe an eighth-assed plan."

For a boy filled with crazy-ass ideas, Dodge was quick to judge.

"Here's how we'll do it, Numbster," said Dodge.

Nate swallowed hard. He listened to the wind, wanting to hear Dodge Hoebeek explain a better way out of this mess. Nothing came, just the bite of a storm front moving in.

The alternative to making a run for it was staying here, next door to two criminals who apparently weren't happy with him being around — as in *existing*. They'd been in jail. He wasn't sure for what. Didn't want to think about it.

He piled a third load of wood inside the cabin. He filled the box and was stacking the logs against the wall, just about finished, when the stranger appeared again. He entered without knocking, his ski mask still in place. One of his eyes was red and watery, but the other was sharp as flint.

"Looks like you're set up good," he said.

Nate glanced at what he'd done. "Yeah, this should be okay."

The man looked toward the kitchen, saw the water buckets by the sink. Nodded.

"Uh, thanks," said Nate.

The man chuckled darkly. "Don't thank me yet, boy," he said. He looked past Nate at the boarded-up picture window. "Since you've got no reason to be hidin' no more, why don't you take down them shutters — get yourself some real honest-to-God sunlight in here, what there is of it."

"Yeah. That would be good."

"Okay," the man said. He almost sounded friendly. He stood there looking around, taking in the camp. "Amazing you survived that boating incident," he said. Nate didn't speak. He wasn't about to tell the man who he truly was — where he truly belonged. "Yep, your family — what's left of it — must have been real relieved to see you." He stared at Nate, sticking out his chin in expectation of a response. None came. He shook his head. "Damn fool gamble, if you ask me."

Nate cleared his throat. The guy wasn't going to quit until he said something. "Yeah. My dad really blew it."

The man sniggered. "Hell, you can say that again. Stupid chump. Course it wasn't just him."

"What do you mean?"

The stranger smiled behind his black mask, revealing that glint of gold again. "I'd have thought you'd know," he said. Then, for the second time in less than an hour, he took his leave, chuckling to himself as he closed the door behind him.

Nate stood there seething. Somehow this guy knew he wasn't Dodge, but instead of calling him on the lie, the man had poked at him with a stick — tried to get a rise out of him. He settled down. There were more important matters to attend to. Waiting just long enough for the stranger to make it back to the other camp, Nate ran to the door and opened it carefully, stepped out onto the stoop. The man was nowhere around. So far, so good. He could commence Operation Polaris right away. He turned back into the house to get his outdoor gear and was shutting the door when he stopped in his tracks. Slowly he turned around to look out at the stoop. His snowshoes and poles were gone.

Okay, get a grip. It wasn't far to the snowmobile shed. It would take a good few minutes to get there in snow that had drifted up to his waist in places. So all it meant was that he would need to start off earlier. No big deal. And when he got to the trailhead, he'd have to drive the Polaris right down to the track since he wouldn't be able to walk too well without snowshoes. When the train came, he could pull right up alongside it and climb off the sled onto the step. Leave the sled there, by the tracks. It might be treacherous, but it was doable.

Then again, he'd probably have to drive along the railbed — keep moving — until the train came. The idea made him go cold inside. There were places where there wasn't much in the way of shoulders to the track; the railbed got so steep, you couldn't ride it, no way. And if a freight train was coming through, a hundred cars long . . . Well, they didn't stop for anything.

"This is officially a sixteenth-assed plan, Numbster."

"Put a sock in it, Dodge!" Nate shouted to the empty house. "If you can't say anything constructive, shut up."

He waited for a comeback. Dodge didn't like to let anyone have the last word. But again, there was only silence.

The Budd car *would* come. And however far he got, it would stop for him. He'd abandon the snowmobile — nothing else he could do. And now he figured his life really was in danger so abandoning it was okay — it wasn't irresponsible. They'd come back for it. Him and his dad. He swallowed hard.

This was not looking good.

He needed food. He needed to be charged up.

There wasn't a lot of choice. The good stuff was at the head of the trail. So it looked like mac and cheese again. Comfort and carbs.

But before he ate, he took Masked Man up on his suggestion. Easing his way around the camp, hard by the walls, he made it to the front, where he took down both of the picture-window sets of shutters. There were four in all, two per window. Back inside, the light made a huge difference. He moved a big easy chair so that it faced south, and ate looking out at the snow-covered lake, sitting beside the fire, piled high and pumping out the heat. Things could be worse. He thought about Dodge out there under all of that whiteness and shuddered.

*Damn fool gamble, if you ask me.*

Yeah. The worst kind of gamble. Gambling away half your family. But what was it he'd said? *I'd have thought you'd know.* What was that supposed to mean?

Nate's meal hardened into a stone in his gut. The light was good but it didn't really change anything. The moment he stepped off that train out at Mile 39, he had entered a white nightmare. Whatever could go wrong probably would.

No! He had to fight that idea.

His eyes wandered over toward the place where he suspected the quadcopter had gone down. The wind was digging into the snow cover as it poured down over the hill, making the trees all around the camp lean and sway. No falling snow yet, just the wind, which seemed to be picking up.

He didn't bother packing.

He filled his pockets with a water bottle, granola bars, and a couple of juice boxes. He found the keys to both the shed and the Polaris in a matchbox in the back of the food cupboard. He dressed up warm again and headed out to make his way across the yard.

You had to take as large a step as you could manage and then kind of dive forward, use your arms to pull your body up out of the snow — swim, crawl if you could, where the crust of an earlier snowfall had been revealed by the wind — then take another step, another dive. After only ten yards, he was already tired. He looked toward the stand of trees that separated the two cabins, expecting to see Masked Man again, enjoying the show. All he could do was keep moving and hoping. The wind in his face didn't help.

And then he was there, though it had cost him a lot of the energy he'd just consumed. His trembling hands dug into his pocket for the shed key. At first, he couldn't find it, and he freaked out thinking it had fallen from his pocket in the perilous journey across the yard. In which case, nobody would find it until spring. But then he laid his hand on the wooden fob and pulled it out. He turned to the doors and stared at the big Yale padlock that held them closed.

Except there were two locks.

The Yale, for which he had the key, and an industrial-grade Master. He pulled on it. It didn't budge. There was no key for a Master lock in the Hoebeeks' place. There had never been a second lock on this door. He undid the Yale, pulled it off. He wasn't quite sure why. Maybe because he'd fought his way here across the snow and this is what he'd come to do. But the Master wasn't going to go away.

And then it dawned on him, something else the masked man had said. *Don't thank me yet, boy.*

# Bird

Nate swore again. He slammed his hand against the doors of the shed. Slammed it again and then looked toward the other camp — his family's camp that his father had built, every damn log of it. The camp where three criminals were holed up, probably having themselves a good old time right about now, laughing themselves sick. The tears came then: tears of rage, tears of exhaustion, tears of fearful loneliness.

He was a prisoner.

He might just as well have been thrown in jail. The snow was as good as any walls if you were trying to pin somebody down, keep them in one place. If he tried to set out for the track right away, he'd be lucky to make it there by one the next morning, by which time he'd have long since died of exhaustion and exposure. Only his ghost self would be standing out there by the tracks waiting for the friendly whistle of the Budd as she came barreling around the bend. He didn't think they stopped for ghosts.

He fumed. Swore a lot. Recovered. Clamped his mouth shut and looked across the yard toward the H-house. He took a deep breath and plunged in. His anger, like a wave, carried him back. He slammed the door and punched the kitchen wall. Then he leaned on the counter and squeezed his eyes shut, trying not to scream.

When he'd gotten himself together, he loaded up the fire and curled up in the ratty old easy chair to look out at the lake.

*What are you doing here?*

He tried to remember how the masked man had said it when he first arrived. He'd sounded surprised to see him. Which was weird, because he'd already guessed someone was in the cabin based on the tracks, the snowshoes outside the door. He knew *someone* was in the building. But he'd been surprised by who he saw, as if he hadn't expected to see Nate. How did he say it? "What are *you* doing here?" Or had it been "What are you doing *here*?"

Whatever he'd said, he knew Nate wasn't Dodge Hoebeek. He seemed to know a whole lot about way, way too much.

Around 1:00 p.m., the old man came around again. It was hard to tell if he was grinning behind his ski mask, but Nate figured he must be.

"Why don't you take that thing off?" said Nate without thinking, too angry to stop himself.

The man stared at him. The rheumy eye looked worse. He blinked, once, twice. "You know who those boys over there are?" Nate didn't answer, but his face must have given something away. "Yeah, I figured as much. You guessed, di'n't ya." It wasn't a question.

Nate thought about it. What more did he have to lose? He nodded.

"Well, that's something. You're not quite as stupid as I thought.

So, here's the deal, kid. You play this right and you just might get out of this mess alive. And when you do, you'll have yourself a story to tell. But see, I don't want to be part of that story. I don't want you givin' no description of the third man in the operation. Y'hear me?"

Nate nodded.

The man nodded back. He was leaning, his hand on the counter, favoring the leg that made him limp.

"Seems like you took a little stroll," he said, barely keeping the laughter out of his voice. "How was that for you?"

Nate toyed with the idea of telling the man where he could shove his ski mask. Instead, he just turned toward the window and looked out at the lake, his hands stuck deep in his pockets, watching the snow stirred up into a fury now by the incessant wind out of the north. A wind that was bringing nothing but trouble.

"Eh?" said the man. "You waiting on that de Havilland Beaver with your weekend buddies onboard?" Nate didn't turn, didn't answer. "Man, oh man, I'd love to see Chuck Belanger wrestle that plane down into this wind."

Nate stared through slits out at the snow racing away from him toward the islands and the narrows. This guy knew everyone. Everything.

"Assuming Chuck was even around. Which he ain't, by the by; he's down in Florida. Smart man." He waited, and now Nate couldn't talk even if he'd wanted to because tears were seeping from his eyes. Partially it was at the news that there was no one at Lauzon, so his dad wouldn't be coming in by plane even if he had gotten the message. And partially because every lie he'd come up with was being thrown back in his face, one by one.

"I'm talking to you, boy," said the man, his voice surly again. "Dodge," he said, with no attempt to conceal his scorn.

Nate just stared out at the day clouding over, obliterating the sun, bringing with it another night in this place of memories he didn't want to have to deal with. The man strode across the room, and before Nate could do more than hunch his shoulders, the guy had his neck in a vise-like grip from behind.

"You should be polite to your elders, kid." The words came out like bullets from between his teeth. "I saved your scrawny ass just now, whether you know it or not."

Nate reached up with both his hands to try to release the man's grip on his neck.

"Let me go!"

But the man bent down close to his ear, close enough for Nate to smell his breath; it was as if a muskrat had crawled into the guy's mouth and died. Then with one more pincer-like squeeze, the stranger let go, pushing Nate's head forward so that his face almost smashed into the windowsill.

Nate swung around to look at the man. "You're pretty tough for a guy who hides behind a mask."

The slap came out of nowhere, so lightning fast Nate couldn't have ducked if he'd tried. His face twisted in agony. His cheek burned. New tears threatened but he forced them back. He wasn't going to give this man the satisfaction. But when he reached up to feel his cheek, he realized that his face was already filmed with wetness.

The stranger stepped back. "I come over to make sure you wasn't hatchin' no more little plans." He waited. His voice didn't sound so harsh anymore. He was breathing hard, as if maybe the slap had taken something out of him. "Like I told ya, those boys over there . . . man, you do *not* want to mess with 'em. You try any other stunts like that . . . well, I won't be able to do nothin' for you." Again, he waited. What was he waiting for, another thank you?

Nate took his chances and turned away again. "Ya hear me?" said the man, coming nearer, lowering his voice as if there were people nearby listening. "You keep quiet. Keep your head down. And like I said, you just might make it out of here alive. You got that?"

Nate turned to look at him. "Got it."

"Good." The man's hard hands rubbed the wool of his mask as if it were itching his face something terrible. He rubbed the wetness out of his bad eye. Nate wasn't fool enough to mistake the moisture for tears. He straightened up, stretched a crick out of his back, and turned to leave. "The Bird just saved your bacon. Don't forget that."

"What?"

"You wanted to know who I am? The Bird, that's who. All you need to know." He limped toward the door.

Nate's mind was racing. *A chance to get out of here without the bird.* He had thought they were talking about the helicopter. But . . .

"They want to get rid of you, too," said Nate.

The man stopped. He turned around slowly.

"What's that?"

Nate stood up and faced him. "When I first got here, I spied on the camp over there. One of them had been up the hill to this old miner's cabin. You can get recep—"

"Yeah, yeah, I know the place. What'd you *think* you heard them say?"

Nate stared the stranger in the eye. With the light on his covered face, Nate could see the glint there. "The one who stayed at the camp came out to meet the other guy. He said he'd talked to someone named Kev?" Nate waited. The man gave nothing away. "Anyhow, the guy said 'they' couldn't come. But there was a chance the guys could get out without the bird. Something like that." He paused and then, as if Dodge were right there whispering in his ear, he said something else. "They made it sound like they really didn't like you much."

Just reading his body language, it was possible for Nate to see that his words had landed.

"You're full of crap."

"No, I'm not," said Nate, feeling bold. "At first I thought they were talking about the chopper — like a whirlybird. They weren't. Those guys don't need you. Not anymore."

The next thing Nate knew, he was falling back into his chair with the man hovering over him, one hand on each of the easy chair's armrests, his face inches from Nate's. "Wha' do you know?"

"I only know what I heard," said Nate.

"I wanna hear everythin'!"

Nate turned his face away. The stench of the man was making him gag. An insane fantasy came to him: he'd deposited the filleting knife down the side of the easy chair and now all he had to do was pull it out and thrust it up into the man's guts. His belly was right there! So close. Nate could imagine the thin blade slicing up through the man's bib overalls, slicing into his flesh, his innards, so that they spilled out all over him like in a scene from *The Walking Dead*. He shuddered, had to fight the urge to throw up.

The man pulled away, but didn't walk away. He stood, his arms crossed. "Talk to me," he said.

Nate looked up at him. Looked into his eyes, one clear, one not. There was something going on here, something he didn't understand. This guy was not like the other two. He was nasty, all right, but Nate had obviously struck a nerve. He might get himself slapped again, but this man might be the closest thing he had to an ally.

"Those are the guys who escaped from the Sudbury Jail,

right?" The man neither nodded nor shook his head. "I recognized them from TV. Anyway, I've been thinking about what they said." He paused, swallowed. "They were hoping for the helicopter to come for them, but it couldn't. I'm guessing that's because of the storm."

Nate looked at the masked face, trying to assess if the man was going to lash out at him again. "When I was getting the water, I noticed a round kind of hollow in the snow. And I wondered if it was like the . . . I don't know, the downdraft from a helicopter."

"The rotor wash."

"Yeah. And I remembered watching the video of the men trying to climb into the helicopter, and it was just hovering there, stationary, and it dawned on me that that's how they got here. They were dropped off, but the helicopter couldn't land on account of the snow."

The masked man sniffed, rubbed his nose. "More like what might be under the snow," he said.

"Solid ice."

"Maybe, maybe not. Anyway, copter pilots don't like what they can't see. This time of year — and this close to shore — there'll sometimes be slush under the snow sittin' on top of the ice." He stopped and cussed, as if he'd said too much.

Nate picked up where he'd left off. "So from what they said, I figured they were either going to have to wait out the storm and then clear a spot on the ice, or get out some other way. And you *were* the only other way out. But maybe not anymore."

"You're full of it."

"Maybe. But you're the one who found them this place, aren't you? It was a place you knew about — I don't know how." Nate waited a moment, but it was unlikely this guy was going to tell him anything more. "Except that now it sounds like they've found some *other* guy who can help them get out of here and bypass you. Cut you out."

The man looked at the lake, dabbed at his rheumy eye again. It was leaking bad. He scratched his arm, tapped his foot. And a strange thought occurred to Nate. It was as if now, this man, the Bird, were somehow a prisoner as well.

# The Remington

If he was going to have to stay the night in a house next door to two criminals with their boxers in knots, Nate decided he had better get out of his funk and do some planning.

Which meant sleeping upstairs, first and foremost.

There were three small rooms. The best one for his purposes was probably Dodge's because of the attic above the bunks. He climbed up on the top bunk and pushed at the trapdoor. It was tight; he had to put his back into it. There wasn't a full attic, just a crawl space, and there was no real flooring, just a couple of planks laid across the rafters, one to either side of the opening. Even before the Hoebeeks moved in, Dodge had plans for that attic crawl space.

"We're going in." Dodge stares at the new camp under construction. His family is living in a couple of tents this summer — truly camping out — sharing the facilities at the Crows' place. But everyone's gone on an expedition this fine morning, except for him and Nate. The camp was supposed to be finished by early July, but with one thing and another, it's still a work in progress. The work crew is also gone for the day, down to the south end.

"We're not supposed to," says Nate.

"Oh, my dear old wussy Numbster. 'Not supposed to' — right there's the difference between the exhilaration of discovery and total boredom." It makes Nate think of those inspirational posters they have up in the guidance counselor's office, usually involving cats. Meanwhile, Dodge has found an aluminum ladder and is manhandling it into position to get up to the second floor in the absence of any stairs.

"What don't you understand about the words 'strictly forbidden'?" says Nate.

Dodge pulls the rope to raise the ladder a few more notches until it leans against the header of the landing. He stops, looks thoughtful for a moment, as if it's a question worth considering. "Well," he says. "'Strictly' speaking, 'forbidden' is one of those past . . . whatchamacallits?"

"What do you mean?"

"You know, in grammar — a past particle."

"Participle?" says Nate. "And stop pretending to be a dumbass."

"That's it, a past participle. 'Forbidden' is a *past* participle. Right?"

Nate frowns, not sure if it is or isn't. "What are you talking about?"

"If my mom said, 'I strictly *forbid* you to go on the construction site,' I'd have to obey her. But by saying it was 'strictly forbidden,' she actually only meant it *was* something she *used* to think I shouldn't do."

Nate stares at Dodge in wonder. "You know what you're full of, right?"

Dodge starts up the ladder. He nods. "Hey, my dad taught me everything I know."

They find themselves in the room directly across from the landing — the one that's going to be his. The hole for the attic gapes at them, too inviting to pass up. It's hot, and when they maneuver a couple of sawhorses and two-by-fours into place so they can poke their heads through the attic opening, it's like a sauna.

"Like putting your head into a pot of soup," says Nate.

But Dodge isn't listening. "We can hide stuff here, man."

"Like what?"

"Contraband. Booze. Girls!"

Nate makes a face. Girls have only just come onto his radar and he's keeping a wide berth. To hear Dodge talk, he's a lot further ahead in his explorations, with someone named Ashley; someone named Skylar; someone named Brynn.

"They'd melt," says Nate, wiping the sweat out of his eyes.

"Melting's good," says Dodge, nodding, lost in some dreamy reflection. Nate huffs and climbs down to the floor, which is where he is when he hears Fern Hoebeek bellowing from below, clearly back way earlier than expected.

"There better not be any foolhardy boys in this house or there's going to be hell to pay!"

Nate stood on the top bunk, head and shoulders through the opening. Which made it pretty easy to hoist yourself in, if need be. It sure wasn't hot up there now. It would only be way colder and way darker come nightfall. And although heat rises, he doubted it would be too comfortable if he ended up hiding there for any length of time. A last resort, maybe. He decided to store a couple of blankets and a pillow, just in case. He was about to climb back down when he saw something shadowy in the corner. He pulled himself through the hole and slithered in far enough to grab what he knew by then to be a book. It was one of the *Diary of a Wimpy Kid* sequels. Trick loved them. There was a bookmark in it about ten pages from the end. For a moment Nate wondered if Trick had discovered the attic. But Trick was not allowed in his big brother's room under penalty of death. Then he remembered something else, a whole other day, years after the construction-site incident. Just last summer, in fact. He swallowed. It was the first time he'd thought about the new meaning of "last summer."

"Where is it?"

"Where's what?"

"My book."

Trick stands on the Hoebeeks' deck with his hands on his hips: he's a toothpick in a ball cap and swimsuit. Dodge is lounging on a deck chair playing *Angry Birds 2* on his iPad.

"What book?" says Nate.

"The new Wimpy Kid. He stole it!"

"For your own good, Patrick. You're already too much of a wimp."

"Am not."

"'Am not,'" says Dodge, making his voice all high and squeaky. Trick grabs at the iPad and Dodge cuffs his hand away.

"Ow!"

"See what I mean? Wimp."

"Give him the book," says Nate.

"Nuh-uh. He reads way too much. And when he reads those

books, he goes, 'Oh, goody, goody, there are other wimpy kids out there just like me so it's okay to be one, too.'"

"That is so much horse manure," says Nate, laughing.

"Next he'll be reading about how it's okay to be gay," says Dodge.

Nate throws himself back in his chair, groaning. "Are you really as big a bigot as you pretend to be?"

"The totally biggest."

Trick is about to speak and then can't. He reaches into his pocket and pulls out his inhaler. Takes a couple of puffs.

"Wimp," says Dodge.

"I'm telling Mom," says Trick.

"Wimp, wimp, wimp," says Dodge.

Then suddenly Trick darts forward and smacks the iPad right out of his brother's hands. It clatters to the deck.

Trick backs away. Nate sits up, ready for anything. Dodge doesn't move. He stares straight ahead, out at the lake. His hands tighten on the arms of the chair.

"I'm sorry," says Trick in his wimpiest voice.

"Not as sorry as you're going to be," says Dodge.

Then Trick disappears. Vanishes. Goes up in smoke. Nate doesn't know which; he's too busy watching Dodge, who sits perfectly still. Then, after a moment, his grip on the chair slackens. The muscles in his face relax. He reaches down lazily and picks up the iPad.

"Do you believe that?" he says, starting up the game again.

"No," says Nate. "I don't."


The second-floor landing was small, but there was room enough under the north-facing window for the big old steamer trunk, where the family kept their extra bedding. Taking it out, Nate lifted the trunk on end and jostled it over to the stairwell. He found that it fit nicely between the wall and the rail, with a narrow space beside that he could squeeze through as need be. If push came to shove — literally — he could heave the trunk down on top of someone charging up the stairs. It was heavy even without its contents. Nate planned to put it in place before he went to bed.

Downstairs, he rigged up something to make a lot of noise if someone came barging in. That was easy: he found the cowbell Fern Hoebeek used to call her brood home for dinner. It usually hung on a hook outside the door; now it was on a shelf just inside. Nate attached it to a string, then to a chair, looped the string over a nail in the beam above, and connected the string to the door. He tried it, opened the door.

*Clang.*

Worked just fine. He also laid a couple of chairs on their side in the path of the door as well. A little clatter could only help.

There had to be other deterrents. He came up with one or two. It was the best he could do.

Was he really preparing for an attack?

He made his way to the master bedroom, on the first floor just off the living room. In the closet, he found the last thing he needed — the very last thing. It was standing in a corner, safe in its tough polyester case with the thick foam padding: Art Hoebeek's Remington Wingmaster, a 12-gauge pump action. The case was locked, and the key for it was not with the other keys but on the highest shelf of the pantry, in the back corner in a tin marked BAK-ING SODA, out of reach of little fingers. Nobody wanted Patrick, let alone baby Hilton, playing with guns, after all. The shotgun also had a trigger lock, opened with a combination of numbers — Art Hoebeek's idea of maximum security. Like everything else about this place, Nate knew what that combination was.

Nate stood in the darkening master bedroom caught in another memory — they were thick on the ground here. Well, that wasn't really surprising.

It was three or four summers back: Mr. H. teaching him and Dodge how to use the Remington. Burl Crow was the woodsman of the north end, but he wasn't into guns. He'd done his share of hunting — had nothing against it. He just didn't want firearms around the camp. Art didn't share Burl's view, so the two fathers agreed to disagree. Which is why the training session happened on one of those rare summer weeks when Burl was back in the city. Nate remembered feeling a bit like a traitor. But he also remembered the satisfaction of blasting a target right off its post.

He woke into the dark to the sound of the wind, howling now. He sat up, listening hard, trying to pick out a sound inside of it. God, it was so loud he wondered if he'd even hear the cowbell. He kicked off his covers and climbed down from the top bunk. He approached the starry window, thick on the inside with frost. He cleared a patch of glass with his hand and looked out into the night. Shivered. Somewhere up in the cloud cover a moon was shining, though there was no sense of its shape or actual where-abouts, only a diffuse glimmer. He would need to go down and fuel the fire, but he was too tired, his body too heavy with sleep. Gradually his eyes accustomed themselves to the expanse before him, and there, down on the shoreline, stood Dodge.

He was bathed in blue light. He was carrying the shotgun.

By the time Nate beat it down to him by the slapping tide, it was a hot, still summer afternoon. Time had blown away the north wind and they were thirteen.

"What are you doing with that?"

Dodge holds the Remington to his shoulder like a Revolutionary minuteman and peers along the stock. "We're about to rid Picnic Island of the menace that has afflicted our summer vacation."

"You're crazy. What are you talking about? And point that thing someplace else!" Nate steers the muzzle away from him.

"You know what I'm talking about."

Nate sighs. He has an idea, but that isn't the point. "Dodge. You're not supposed to be playing with that thing."

"It's a gun, Nate, not a thing."

"You know what I mean."

Dodge gives him a sour expression and lowers the weapon. "Listen, our moms have taken my little bros down to Sanctuary Cove. They won't be back until supper. Your dad won't be back until tomorrow, and my dad is back in sweet home Indiana selling shit. This is our chance to do something for Our People — make Picnic Island great again!"

Nate sighs. There is no defeating Dodge, no matter how harebrained the scheme. And Nate figures it's probably better if he's along for the ride. He looks out at the lake. It's dead calm — a perfect green mirror. He shields his eyes. If you look far enough, and have an eye for it, there is a line maybe two or three hundred yards out where the turbulence begins, but it doesn't look too rough today.

"Okay, I'll get the life jackets." Nate glares at Dodge to make his point. The thing is, neither motorboat is there, so they are going to have to paddle. And the rippled water farther out is just that, nothing they haven't handled a million times before, but more worrying this time with the cargo they have onboard. Nate, who is lighter than Dodge, sits in the bow. Dodge sits in the stern, singing some stupid song, oblivious to the bumping of the waves against the prow, while Nate imagines them going over with every seventh slap. Not a big deal, normally. There'd been loads of times when they'd *deliberately* rocked the canoe over for the fun of it and then practiced clambering back onboard. But that was the kind of horsing around you did nearer shore, not out here. He glanced behind him at the black polyester bag.

"I'm worried about the rifle."

"It's not a rifle, Numbster."

"The *gun.*"

"Just paddle, we're almost there."

For the rest of the journey, all Nate can think about is capsizing and the gun falling slowly, end over end, down, down, down in its polyester casket, disappearing at last into the deeper greenness of the trench where the biggest lake trout lurk.

They make it.

"Of course we made it!" says Dodge, leaving Nate to pull the canoe up onto the sloping ledge of the island. "Now let's go kill us some *hive!*"

There is a huge wasp nest hanging from a branch high above the picnic table. The table has been there forever. It looks as if it could fall apart any moment just from the number of names etched into its mold-mottled surface by who-knew-how-many pocketknives. It's a communal place, a lunchtime stop-off for fishing parties. There's even an improvised filleting table suspended between two trees, to clean fish for a fry-up. The Northenders have had to avoid the picnic spot all summer.

"Be ready to run," says Nate, looking up into the tree and the wasps circling their monstrous gray home. It's grown bigger, like some huge evil piñata.

"We've got the lake twenty yards away, man. We're good." Dodge is aiming the shotgun.

"Yeah, well just don't miss," says Nate.

"Oh, ye of little faith," says Dodge, and fires.

The noise is huge and he doesn't miss. The hive explodes into the kind of confetti you'd only see at a ghoul's wedding. Nate runs like a scalded cat, only turning as he reaches the water's edge to see Dodge still standing by the picnic table, watching the hive-dust fall like filthy snow and the whirling tornado of angry wasps.

"DODGE! RUN!"

And finally he does, stooping to drop the Remington onto a bed of mossy ground, laughing his fool head off, diving into the lake and going way under, Nate by his side, two dolphins. When they surface fifty yards out, they tread water, watching the scene on the beach.

"It's going to be fall by the time we can get the gun," says Nate.

"Maybe," says Dodge, "but it was fun, wasn't it?"

And Nate, recovering now, safe and distant from the buzzing chaos of those angry vespids, has to nod. Yeah, it's fun in a heart-stopping way. Dodge kind of fun.


He woke shivering on the lower bunk. When he'd gone back to bed, the idea of climbing to the top had seemed beyond him. Light as weak as skim milk sifted through the window. There was no sky, only snow now. Snow falling sideways, churned by the relentless wind.

On the landing, he shouldered the on-end trunk aside, like it was the mighty door of a castle keep, to make his way downstairs. He dressed quickly by the fire in the same clothes he'd put on in his bedroom back home two days ago: thick socks — now dry again, but getting stiff — long johns, snow pants, turtleneck, and a down vest. It was Saturday. No train south today. He stoked the fire and stood by it, letting the heat dig out the shivers. He looked out at the day, and through the swirling white blizzard he saw someone on the ice. It was one of the guys — Shades, he figured, but he couldn't tell because he had his back turned and his hood up. He was out way beyond the water hole, which Nate couldn't see from this angle. He was just standing there, looking down, his hands in his jacket pockets. Nate went cold all over. It was around there somewhere that the quad had crashed. But how . . .

The man stepped aside, as if he somehow knew Nate was watching and he was moving to let him see.

The wind had partially dug out the drone.

One black rotor on the otherwise white copter had been revealed. The thing was so light it would have blown away across the frozen lake if its bottom half hadn't been trapped in the snow. This one telltale corner. Now the man squatted and started digging with his hands to liberate it.

He stood, uncoiling himself, and he turned. Shades, all right, in his wraparound sunglasses, staring toward the Hoebeeks' camp, a big grin on his face, the toy in one hand, the other held out as if to say, "Now what have we here?"

"Oh crap."

Nate stepped away from the window, staring at nothing, his mind as frozen as the landscape outside. This was not going to go well.

# Bird Revealed

It was difficult to tell at first that the thumping on the back door was made by the flat of a human hand and not just the wind. The wind had wanted in the whole time Nate had been holed up at the Hoebeeks', first from the front and now from the back. Like a living thing, it was circling the house, looking for any weakness. The noise down there now was not the weather come a-calling; it *was* a living thing — an angry living thing.

Nate stood at the top of the stairs with the "gate closed." The heavy trunk sat ready, slightly over the lip of the top step. He was prepared to tip it at a moment's notice. Too bad he didn't have a cauldron of hot tar.

*Smash!*

The locked door crashed open and set the cowbell clanging and the chairs clattering. Nate couldn't see the entranceway from where he stood, but he heard first one chair, then another skitter across the floor as if they had been kicked, and then . . . wait for it . . .

*Thump!*

The sound of a body meeting the floor — a body that had stepped into a freshly poured pool of very old, slightly rancid, recently melted vegetable oil. He couldn't see the man, but he did see a pair of silver sunglasses skitter across the oily floor.

"My goodness," said the man. "You're just *full* of surprises, aren't you?"

The tone of his voice was light, bantering and terrifying. Nate wondered whether the oil had been a good idea.

He heard Shades clamber to his feet and then appear below, picking up his glasses. He rubbed the lenses across his sleeve and, taking a look, wagged his head in dismay. "These are *Guccis,*" he said to the open space. "Cost me an arm and leg. Not *my* arm, mind you. Not *my* leg. The guy I took them from. He wasn't going to need them anymore."

He unzipped his coat and shoved the glasses in the chest pocket of his shirt. Nate watched through the crack between the trunk and the banister. The man looked straight ahead, then walked farther into the camp. He took off his grease-stained jacket and hung it over the back of one of the dining room chairs. He was wearing Astrid's scarf, the one he'd been wearing when Nate first saw him. Now he unwound it, slowly, coil by coil, as if he were planning on a long stay. In profile, Nate could see an impressive multicolored tattoo on the guy's neck: an eagle in a dive, a raptor's glint in its eye, its wing tips curling up behind the man's ear and its talons poised for prey. Shades rounded the corner into the living room and disappeared from Nate's view. He heard the master bedroom door open and shut with a click a moment later. Soon enough, Shades was back and standing at the bottom of the stairs. Nate had ducked out of sight just as he came into view.

"Now isn't that an imposing sight! A barricade." Nate was out of sight behind the big blue-and-brass trunk, waiting. Ready. But he wasn't ready for what he heard next. A sound he'd never heard in real life but knew instantly what it was: a handgun being cocked. "Let me tell you about this firearm," said the man. "It's loaded with some super-duper bullets. Teflon coated. You ever hear of such a thing?" He made extravagant lip-smacking sounds, as if he'd just taken a bite of lemon meringue pie. "The improvements these manufacturers get up to," he said. "*Very* impressive."

Then he took a step up the stairs.

"Now, some people call these here bullets 'cop killers' because they're really good at piercing car doors." He chuckled. "Have I got your attention yet?"

Behind the man, the wind howled through the door he'd left open, which kept banging against the wall, kept the cowbell clanging. Nate slid to the floor as if a silent bullet had already pierced the trunk and brought him down.

"I'd like to meet you, young man," said Shades. "Preferably *before* I kill you. Because I have a question or two to ask." He paused, then Nate heard him take another step up. Nate slid away from the trunk on his belly, but not so far that his feet lost contact with it.

"Are you being coy with me? Hard to get?" The man waited. "Oh, please," he said, a note of irritation finally finding its way into his chatty voice. "Why don't you just come on down!" He put some energy into the last words, as if he were a host on the worst possible game show ever.

Nate felt Dodge stirring inside him. *Really? You think I'm coming down there?* But there was no Dodge to give him the bravado to say anything at all.

"You see, we really, really want to know what you've been up to! Before, as I said, I waste you."

If they'd found the cell phone, they'd know exactly what Nate had been up to. But maybe it had fallen off and sunk into the snow, or was frozen and they couldn't fire it up? Either way, he wasn't going to respond. He doubted if his voice would make it through an entire sentence.

"Oh man. I am getting *so* bored," said Shades. "And I've got to tell you, I am losing my patience."

"You never had much to begin with," said a voice Nate recognized. And then the door finally closed, tight, and the cowbell stopped clanging.

"Stay out of this, Bird."

"Thought you said you was goin' to the outhouse, Shaker. Then I found myself wonderin' why a man'd take a handgun to the outhouse."

"I *said* stay out of this."

"No, you stay out of this. You don't want no more trouble 'n you've got already on your plate."

The man called Shaker sighed. "Oh, how little you know me."

Nate dared to peer around the trunk and saw, for the first time, the revolver in Shaker's hand: black with maybe a six-inch barrel. Shaker was looking at Bird, but then he turned toward the stairwell and Nate's head darted back behind the upended trunk. "I'm going to count to three," said Shaker. "I can count a lot higher than that, but three is about the limit of my patience right now."

"Leave the kid alone."

"One —"

"Put that damned thing away," said Bird, more irritated than anything else.

"Wait your turn, Bird. Let me kill the boy first and *then* you."

"And leave you stranded," said Bird. "It's as much as you deserve." And then he entered farther into the camp.

"Don't step in the oil!" Nate shouted.

The footsteps stopped abruptly. "What the hell?"

He must have assessed the situation. Maybe he noticed Shaker's pants all greased and streaky, the coat hanging over the back of the chair even worse off. Because the next thing Nate heard was the old guy laughing.

"Oh please!" said Shaker. "Don't encourage the brat."

"Just put the gun down," said Bird calmly. "Beck's gone up the hill. He's gonna let Kev know we're comin' out. Within the hour. Ya hear what I'm sayin'? You don't need this." Nate dared to peek.

"Oh, it isn't about need!" said Shaker, holding his handgun at face height. "This is all about *want*. I've been cooped up in this damn wilderness hovel for days now and I'm just dying to blow somebody's head off."

"Well, if you like," said the old man. "Here, let me help."

There was a skittering noise — one of the chairs — and suddenly there was a thud, one very similar to what Nate had heard five minutes ago. He peered around the corner of the trunk and saw Shaker lying on the floor again, a chair having taken his feet out from under him. Bird was standing over him. Bird had a rifle he was holding the wrong way around, the butt suspended above his victim's face. The handgun lay on the floor, hefty and deadly looking.

"It looks like I'm going to have to see my chiropractor when I get out of here," said Shaker, rubbing his shoulder. He lay his head back on the shiny wet floor and swore mightily, like someone hoping to pop nails out of the rafters with his voice. It was the first time Nate had heard him raise his voice, and the change—the rage—in it froze him to the core.

"We. Don't. Need. This," said Bird, leaning over him.

Shaker glared up at him and then, with surprising speed, grabbed his handgun and had it aimed at Bird's chest before the old man could do a thing. "Drop it," said Shaker, all the fake friendliness gone from his voice.

Very slowly and carefully, Bird lay the rifle down on the floor while Shaker hitched himself up on his free elbow and then gradually climbed to his feet, never taking his eye off the man in the ski mask. "I'm really tired of you telling me what to do, old man. You got us into this godforsaken hole. And now look what's happened."

"Nothin's *happened*!" said Bird. "We're stuck in a storm is all. The copter couldn't come back for you."

"Yeah, well, some of us wonder why it had to leave in the first place."

"You know damn well why."

"Bird, please face facts: the plan stinks."

"The plan is your get-out-of-jail card. In another couple weeks, in case you forgot, you was gonna be shipped south to a nice, cozy maximum-security penitentiary. For twenty years. So, yeah, the storm is inconvenient. Believe me, I'm as anxious as you to move things along, but we're still good."

Shaker laughed. "Your idea of good is *not* my idea of good. And that brat up there . . ." He waved his free hand toward the staircase.

"I'm your option B," said Bird patiently. "Just like before. The roads were all closed off, just like was expected, and so the copter beat it up here. No one has a clue where you are."

"True, neither do we."

"Which is where I come in."

"Which is why the whole thing stinks."

"Whatever," said Bird. "The thing is, the kid makes no difference one way or the other. He'll make a *big* difference if he's dead."

Then the back door opened, the cowbell clanged again, the wind howled. Nate could see none of that from where he hid, but judging by the lack of response from the two men, he assumed it had to be Worried Man, aka Beck, who closed the door and stomped his feet.

"What's going on?" he said.

"Your pal here has the idea that shootin' up the joint might make things better somehow."

"Jesus, Shaker."

"Oh, don't *you* start! I'm so tired of this. Tired of him, tired of you, tired of Mr. *Home Alone* up there. Tired of being cooped up. I. Want. Out. Now." He sounded dangerously close to snapping. He poked the gun threateningly at Bird, who held his hands up lazily but otherwise did not back away.

"What's the news?" said Bird. "You get through to your people?"

Beck moved into view below. He picked up Bird's rifle from the floor, strapped it over his shoulder, and walked around to stand behind Shaker. "Yeah. They're going to meet us at the lumber camp."

"In *this*?" said Shaker, waving his arm toward the window, the storm.

"They got one of them snowcats with the enclosed cab," said Beck. "Storm's no problem. They'll be there for us."

"See? What'd I tell you," said Bird, his voice unperturbed. "So why don't we just get back to camp, get ourselves sorted out, and hit the trail."

"Kev say anything else?" said Shaker.

Beck nodded, smiling nervously. "Yeah. It's just like I was telling you."

Now Shaker smiled, too. "Good. Good. That's the best news I've heard in days."

Bird put his hands on his hips, bowed his masked head, and shook it slowly. "Here we go," he said. "I heard you cowboys might be cookin' something up."

"Whadaya mean?" said Beck.

"A little birdie told me."

"What?" said Beck.

"I think he means the annoying little villain hiding upstairs," said Shaker.

"What'd he tell you?" said Beck.

Bird sighed. "That your good pal Kev had a plan to cut me out. Save your people payin' the money they owe me for holin' you up while the heat was on and gettin' you out when the time comes. Which, apparently, is now."

"There you go," said Shaker, sounding pleased. "We're done here." Without taking his eyes off Bird, he inclined his head toward his partner. "So let me deal with this riffraff and we'll go, right?"

"Yeah . . . well, it's not that easy," said Beck.

"What do you mean?" asked Shaker, which made Bird chuckle. "Oh, shut up!" said Shaker, and reaching out, he grabbed the top of the man's ski mask and tore it off his head. Then he threw it on the floor.

From where Nate stood, he couldn't make out much: black

thinning hair, going gray at the temple, a face as much like wood as his gnarly hands. Pockmarked skin. A bent nose — probably from sticking it so often into other people's business.

"I want to take a good long look at your ugly mug before I reconfigure it," said Shaker. "Man, I have *really* been waiting for this. You and then the brat."

"Cut it out," said Beck, his voice panicky. "You don't want any more blood on your hands."

"What have I got to lose? You got directions, right?"

"Yeah, well . . . like I said."

"What?"

"I'll tell you what," said Bird, "since your pal here ain't exactly forthcomin'. Kev couldn't help you out with directions. Could he, Beck? No need to answer. GPS'd be useless, since there's no reception in the bush. So I'm guessing he said something like follow *my* snowmobile trail out and then . . . what? Take a hard left at the 7-Eleven? Maybe drop in and get some cash from the ATM nailed onto a tree up by the Spanish River while you're at it?"

"Didn't I tell you to shut up?" said Shaker.

Bird chuckled again. "Think about it. My trail will have been wiped out by this blizzard. And even if you *could* follow it to where I come in, there's a whole lot more forest between there and Branigan's lumber camp, assumin' that's where this pickup of yours is supposed to happen. And that forest out there, boys, in case you didn't notice, goes all the way to James Bay, just about. True, it thins out once you hit the tree line, but take my word for it, *nothing* Kev told you will keep you from getting lost out there until the Second Coming."

Shaker growled low in his throat, then raised the gun as if he were about to pistol-whip Bird, but it was an idle threat. "He send you anything useful, Beck?"

Beck shook his head. "Not really. Bird's right. We need him."

From the look on his face, this was the last thing Shaker wanted to hear. He shook his head. "Well, here's the thing: I'm not sure I do," he said. "Need him, I mean." His voice went deadly quiet. Then he raised his other hand around his gun hand, took one step back, and straightened his arms. "I think this old man walked us right into a trap, and where, pray tell, is he going to take us next?" He held the handgun higher to take aim. "I actually think I don't care." He started to pull back the trigger, when —

"OWWWW!"

The hardball had struck Shaker on the forehead. The scraping sound of the trunk being shoved aside at the top of the stairway had made him turn to look, and Nate had beaned him good. Shaker had been knocked off his feet.

For the third time.

Now Bird stood over him yet again, holding Shaker's firearm, picked up from the floor where it flew when he fell. After a moment, after he'd gotten Beck to hand him back his rifle, Bird shoved the firearm into his overalls pocket, wiping his oily hand on Shaker's pant leg. Meanwhile, Beck crouched beside his partner, resting a hand on his forehead. Shaker slapped it away. The baseball rolled into the living room, pushed by some low gust of wind, looking for all the world as if it were trying to get away.

"Guess this means you get first base for free," said Bird.

Shaker turned his head to glare up the stairs at Nate. Beck looked up at him as well and just shook his head.

"Boy, you are messing with trouble," said Beck.

"You gonna live?" said Bird to Shaker. "'Cause we need to move out. You got that? I'm leadin' ya out and I'm collectin' the money your people owes me. I want to put a whole lotta miles between me and this whole stinkin' business. That's what this is about for me. Gettin' out." He glanced up at Nate, just once, quickly, as if the speech had been aimed his way: some kind of explanation. Then he turned his gaze on the man on the floor. "Your long-sufferin' partner is gonna get you your jacket and you're gonna put it on. He's itchin' to go. Me, too. You want to stay here, it's fine with me. I'll give the boy this fancy Ruger of yours, show him how to use it, in case ya get any more jeezly stupid ideas. Let him finish you off. How's that do ya?"

He glanced up the stairs again. Nate didn't know the face, had never seen it before in his life. But he did half recognize the smile, marred as it was by the leaking eye and the flash of gold and a chipped front tooth. It was a face creviced with age but for the eyes — the one clear eye, anyway. Black as pitch but bright. The Bird, of course: a Crow.

Calvin Crow.

His grandfather.

# Five-Story High

"You've got to be valiant," says Dodge.

"Valiant?" says Nate.

"Yeah, like brave on steroids," says Dodge.

"I know what valiant means," says Nate. "I was just wondering what new hell you're planning."

Dodge grabs him in a head squeeze. "Oh, you know me too well, Master Crow!" Then he steps toward the edge of the cliff and points to the waves slapping far below. "This," he says grandly.

They'd been tromping uphill through the bush to the top of the jumping cliff on the east side of Picnic Island. You could climb up the cliff face maybe twenty or thirty feet from below, but you couldn't scale all the way, not without climbing gear. But they'd found their way in, for the first time, from the picnic spot on the other side of the island. Dodge chuckles. "Bet you don't have the cojones to jump it."

"You're right. And if I did, I'd lose my cojones doing it."

"Told you."

"I'm not going to jump from here because I'm not suicidal," says Nate. He stares down the cliff face, his hands on his hips. "It must be around —"

Dodge cuts him off. "We're not measuring this in yards or feet — and don't give me any of your metric shit, either. This is stories high, Nathaniel; I'd say six, maybe seven. Seven stories."

Nate looks again; his own guess would be closer to five, but that's not what scares him off. The cliff rises from the water at an angle of maybe eighty degrees. He knows the water is plenty deep, even right at the foot of the cliff, but with a slope like this . . . "Man, you'd need to jump out something like three or four yards just to clear the rock face."

"You got it," says Dodge. He looks mesmerized. His expression kind of scares Nate. Then his friend turns his gaze away from the water below. "So we need to make a runway," he says.

They spend a good whack of the afternoon doing just that. Clearing bush in their bathing suits and tees, Nate in his Walmart aqua socks, Dodge in his Speedo Surfwalkers. There is a breeze out near the cliff head strong enough to keep the blackflies at bay, but as they move inland, the flies close around them, getting in their hair and eyes.

Nate knows better than to try to convince Dodge not to do it. So what you do when your best friend is about to try something drastically stupid is make sure the "runway" is clear and long. And you calculate in the back of your head the whole time just how long it will take you to make your way back down, zigzagging through the trees to the boat at the picnic place; get the Evinrude cranked up; and then speed around to the other side of the island to rescue that best friend, who will have hit the stone face of the cliff before making it to the water, maybe gotten himself a concussion and drowned in the meantime.

The runway needs to be straight and, preferably, not uphill. And because of the trees and some intractable undergrowth, they end up with a path that actually runs almost parallel to the cliff for about twenty yards before doglegging right toward the edge for the last ten yards or so. In his mind's eye, Nate imagines a high jumper's approach to the crossbar — coming at it slant.

Nate measures out the stretch directly after the dogleg: five or six good long strides. He stops at the brink, feels a little dizzy looking down. He drinks some water from his bottle. Over to the left, below is a rocky outcrop perfect for mooring the boat when they come out here to jump. It's the same place they stand to operate the Seeker. They've done it all along, daring each other to climb higher and higher but until today only as high as they could make it clawing their way up. If he gives it any thought, Nate can remember seeing Dodge stare up the cliff to the summit more than once. The only surprise is how long it has taken him to think about coming at the cliff from the land side.

They return the next day, set out early with a machete (Dodge) and loppers (Nate), plus an ax and a Swede saw. They are dressed for the bush when they first get there, but as the sun rises, they strip back to the bare essentials, blackflies be damned!

They'd made their way by instinct to the cliff head, finding the path of least resistance, a zigzag path, as it turns out. The island is rocky, with scarcely a rind of soil and clearer of underbrush than the mainland, so by the end of their second day they'd cleared a pretty good pathway from the shoreline on the west side. And now there is this runway to clear, as smooth and free of roots and snags as it can be, so that one crazy-ass best friend can charge toward his doom. That's what's supposed to be the crowning achievement of this second day of grooming. Nate has one other idea to stop Dodge. But he'll have to play it just right.

"Okay, I've enjoyed about as much of this as I can stand," says Dodge, wiping his sweaty face with his forearm. He's covered with dirt and little dots of blood where the vegetation fought back or the blackflies feasted. His ponytail has come undone and his hair is across his eyes and full of twigs. He pulls it tight, replaces the rubber band. "Prepare for liftoff," he says.

It's the perfect segue.

"Hey, wait," says Nate. "Speaking of liftoff, how about we get the quadcopter and film the momentous event. Dodge Hoebeek throws himself off the Empire State!"

You only have to appeal to his vanity to get Dodge's attention.

"Good plan, Numbster," said Dodge, nodding. "Let's do it."

Then he walks to the edge of the precipice. "I'll be back," he says in a bad Arnold Schwarzenegger imitation. As they make their way down the track they've cleared, back to the low side of the island, Nate grins to himself at how easy it has been to escape calamity. At least for now. It's too late to come back today.

A valiant effort.


The door opened. The cowbell was gone. So were the chairs. Nate was washing up the cooking oil on the floor. It was Bird.

Calvin.

"A mop," he said, nodding. "That's more your speed, kid."

"Yeah, well . . ." But Nate didn't want to explain about how you kept the place tidy for next time. Camp was always about next time.

"I'm going to need the keys to the shed and the Polaris," said Calvin.

"You know about that, too?"

Calvin smiled. "You know I do. That extra lock throw you off, kid?"

Nate went back to mopping.

"I make it my business to know everything that goes on down here."

*Up* here, thought Nate. The Northend. But he wasn't about to argue. He looked again at Calvin Crow a moment and then placed the rag end of the mop in the wringer, pushed the handle, and listened to the dirty water drain into the bucket. When it was done, he soaked the mop again and commenced washing the floor.

"I ast you a question, boy. D'ju hear me?"

"You know my name," said Nate without looking up.

"What would that be, Dodge?"

"My real name. You knew it all along."

Calvin sighed impatiently, then leaned against the wall by the door. "Well, you sure as hell ain't that half-wit Hoebeek boy."

"Shut up!"

"Whoa! Easy, now."

"He was my best friend, okay. It's not his fault his father was a fricking lunatic. Dodge would have —"

"Enough!" said Calvin, slicing his hand through the air. "This ain't the time for discussion. The quicker I'm outa here with those hotheads, the better it's gonna be for both of us," said Calvin. "You get that, right?"

Reluctantly, Nate nodded, but the anger raged in him, beating in his head, constricting his throat.

"So whyn't you just give me the damn keys."

Nate stopped again and looked at this man who didn't resemble his father one bit right now. Nate had sure never seen a look of hostility like this on his father's face. And the gleam in the man's eyes was dulled to something dangerous.

"Why'd you never visit?" Nate said.

"Ask your father."

Nate looked away. Shook his head. "You got to admit this is a pretty screwed-up way of meeting for the first time."

Calvin had given him as much time as he was going to. He stood up tall again. "This ain't no jeezly family reunion. The keys. Pronto!"

Nate dared to stand up tall as well. Taller than his grandfather. He shook his head.

"You're Burl's son, all right," said Cal. "Had to knock his head a few times against the wall to get a little respect out of the boy."

"Respect? You call it respect? You almost killed him. The fire that burned down the old camp — if it weren't for him, you'd have been dead."

Calvin laughed. "Oo-ee! I bet you've had an earful of stories about mean old Calvin Crow. Let me tell you —"

"No!" said Nate.

"What'd you say?"

"No," said Nate. "I didn't hear a million stories about you. Just the one. And only when I'd bugged my father over and over. He told me about you burning down the Maestro's place. That's where he got the burn marks on his arms. 'That's all you need to know about your grandfather,' he told me. And so I never asked again."

Calvin nodded, his lips puckered out as if giving this some thought. Then he walked over to Nate and stood across the bucket of dirty water from him and leaned forward. "Without the keys to the shed, I'm going to have to hacksaw that Yale lock off. That's going to take way too much time, and I'm *still* going to need the keys to the friggin' Polaris. So, here's the deal. It would be just as easy — actually, way easier — to take the hacksaw to *you*. Maybe just a finger, maybe a whole hand, dependin' on how pigheaded you wanna be. So I repeat: the keys. Now!"

There was no point in arguing. Nate had seen nothing in the man's eyes to suggest he'd stop short of sawing off his grandson's hand to get what he wanted. He got him the keys.

"Good lad," said Calvin. He headed toward the door but stopped before opening it. "I brought back your snowshoes," he said without turning. "There's food in the fridge over at the other camp. Not that the fridge is on or nothin'; it's cold enough in that sunporch. I know you're gonna want to clean up all nice and pretty after your messy visitors. Might as well enjoy some good grub while you're at it."

Nate swallowed. His instinct was to thank him, despite everything. He fought down that instinct. Calvin turned his way. Nate nodded, stone-faced. Calvin turned again to go, but still he hesitated. Then he turned one more time and the black anger was gone from his face. "I meant what I said back there when the boys was over here. Once I get paid for this business, I'm outa here — out of everyone's hair. Headin' west." He looked around the camp. "Shoulda done it years ago.

"But you can tell your father somethin' for me, okay?"

"What's that?"

"You tell him I always knowed he'd make it — make something out of himself. Knowed it all along. So I'm not gonna apologize for 'sharing' some of what's his. I never had the chances he did. No, sir. What I done . . . let's just call it spreading the wealth. Okay? You got all that?"

It took a moment for Nate to respond. There was too much to digest in what the man said. He nodded anyway. Then the door opened and closed, and Calvin Crow was gone.

# The Threat

Once he'd cleaned the cabin up to within an inch of its life and dumped the dirty water out in the snow and generally made the Hoebeeks' place livable — knowing all along it was unlikely any Hoebeek would ever live there again — Nate stoked the fire and sat cross-legged in the big old easy chair in the living room and watched the snow slash down on ghostly Ghost Lake and tried to put together what had just happened.

What was he supposed to make of a man who had broken into their place — and now the neighbor's place — put Nate's life in jeopardy, then saved his life, in a way, and yet would have been willing to saw off one of his grandson's hands to get what he wanted?

Nate stared at the islands in the narrows, fading out of existence in the snow and failing light as if they were being whisked away to some other place, maybe Neverland. He thought of Dodge

Hoebeek out there somewhere. Maybe that's where he was, too. A cold place, Neverland. Not a place you get any older.

Brave-on-steroids Dodge.

*You sure as hell ain't that half-wit Hoebeek boy.*

Just thinking of what Calvin had said made Nate's blood boil. Where'd he get off talking like that? Yeah, Dodge had gotten them into some tight spots, but nothing they couldn't handle. Nothing *Dodge* couldn't handle. He brought out something wild in Nate. Pushed him. He was intrepid.

Okay, sometimes he was idiotic, when you had the time to think about it. But that was just it — when Dodge was around it was hard to think clearly. He emitted some kind of wave that fried your brain. But also lit it up. Man, he just shone! That's what he did. He burned bright. And he took more space than any normal human being — took more of the air in the room than you did and left you gasping, just trying to keep up. Trick had a puffer he had to use when he couldn't breathe. Asthma, it was supposed to be. But Nate had always wondered if it was just having to live in the same house as Dodge.

His father had warned him about Dodge, pretty well right from the get-go. "You remember yourself, son," Burl had said; that was all he'd said. Remember yourself. What it had meant to Nate was to not let Dodge take you over completely. Not let him change your name on you, make you into something he wanted you to be. And maybe what it had also meant was to remember yourself because Dodge wasn't going to. He was *never* thinking of you, not really. He was generous, in his way, lending you stuff, giving you stuff. But when he set his mind on something — however bat-in-a-shoebox crazy it was — that something was bigger and more important than you were.

Now there was no Dodge left, and Nate did *not* appreciate

some battered old villain bad-mouthing him. Yeah, maybe Dodge was with the Lost Boys dive-bombing Captain Hook, but fantasy aside, he was still alive in Nate's head. He figured Dodge would haunt him forever.

The sound of a snowmobile firing up snapped him from his thoughts. First one, then two, then a third. They were going at last. Had Cal's plans always included stealing the Hoebeeks' Polaris? Maybe not. They could have made do with two sleds. But as luck would have it, Nate showed up. Luck—hah! Or maybe they'd have just torn the place apart to find the keys. Such things didn't seem to matter to Cal Crow, one way or another. There was the Polaris and whatever machine Cal had arrived on, and then there was Burl's vintage Ski-Doo. He wondered which of them would end up with the short straw, riding out on what Dodge had called "your dad's prehistoric vacuum cleaner."

They seemed to have started up the trail, but then one of them must have peeled off because the noise grew louder, and Nate realized it was coming over here. He sat up in his chair.

It's my grandfather, he thought, come to say goodbye.

Then his brain kicked in and he wondered what drug he was on to imagine that that's what was happening. That wasn't going to be Cal arriving at his door. In a flash, Nate was out of his chair, slipping and sliding in his socks and heading up the stairs two at a time. He had only just reached the top when the back door crashed open and the sound of the snowmobile, idling outside the camp, filled the house.

"It's your favorite nightmare!" shouted Shaker in a voice as loud as a dog pound, all smart-ass pretense gone.

He stomped into the camp and, finding no one on the first floor, parked himself at the foot of the stairs. Stomped his feet a few times to make sure Nate knew exactly where he was. Nate was out of sight behind the trunk again, praying he wouldn't come up. "I don't have the time right now, Nathaniel — nice name, by the way — but I wanted to let you know something. I wanted to let you know that if you think you've seen the last of me, you're sadly mistaken." Shaker stepped up onto the first stair. "This shiner on my forehead is a constant, throbbing reminder of you. Do you know what I mean?"

He took another step up. "I could shoot you right through that chest of yours, but I've decided I'd rather wait."

The outside door smacked against the wall, caught in the wind; the snowmobile stuttered. "Waiting builds anticipation. You know what I mean? First, I find my way out of this place, and then, knowing exactly *where* it is, I finds my way back. Easy-peasy." He took another step. "Because you see, Nathaniel, what you've done . . . Well, I'm going to have to mess you up *so* bad that your dear mama won't recognize her little boy."

Then he laughed, stepped back down, and headed out. He slammed the door so hard it broke. That's how Nate found it when the sound of the snowmobile was finally soaked up by the wind and the only thing left outside was the all-consuming storm. The door swung uselessly on its hinges. That creature that had been circling the house had found its way in at last, and now it would devour him. No, it wasn't like that. It was just snow, and all that snow could do was bury you. Already it was drifting through the shattered opening, the wind unrolling a white carpet across the floor. Nate stepped back, felt the wetness on his face, closed his eyes to it, resigned. The last thing he saw was an absence: the snowshoes and poles Cal had left him, sticking in the snow by the stoop, were gone. Again.

# 19

## Snow-Blind

He turned his back on it. Turned his back on the storm pouring into the camp. He walked into the living room and looked out at the lake, what was left of it. Couldn't see the islands or the shores of the bay to either side. The wind he could feel on his back funneling through the open doorway was playing havoc out on Ghost Lake. Maybe it would clear all the snow away, then tear up the ice and with its icy fingers dig Dodge from his silent grave, blow him to kingdom come. He stared into the reeling, whirling whiteness as if expecting at any moment to see him. Dodge, so light he could walk recklessly on air, so porous the wind whistled through him, his hair loose, like yellow fire.

"I loved you, you asshole!"

The tears came and he let them and he let the snow carpet the Hoebeeks' camp because they would never come back and he couldn't stop it anyway. Not the wind or the snow or the feelings that overtook him and were shaking him inside as soundly as the weather. He swayed. Just fall over, he told himself. Just get it over with.

"Wimp," said Dodge. "Numb nuts."

"Stop it!"

Dodge laughed. "Go ahead and die," he said. "I double-dog dare you."

And because it was Dodge and because it was a double-dog dare and because it was more important than anything to do *exactly the opposite* of anything Dodge wanted him to do right now, Nate opened his eyes, seething with anger. He turned and saw the snow creeping up on him across the expanse of open floor, saw it scintillate in the air like radioactive dust while it was already melting into puddles around the woodstove. He swore, big time, so loud it rocked his bones and burned his throat. Then he grabbed the easy chair he'd pulled up to the picture window, grabbed it and, howling with rage, pushed it across the floor like some insane tackle driving a linebacker back from the line of scrimmage.

*Bam!*

The chair plowed into the broken door. And the wind died inside. It still pounded on the door demanding entry. Nate ignored it. What stupid bastard ever listened to the wind?

# Camp

He shoveled and mopped until the H-house sparkled.

"You're such a girl," said Dodge.

"And you're a first-class frigging idiot," said Nate. "A lazy idiot."

"You hear that wind out there, man? We could hitch a sail to the boat and fly!"

Nate managed a tired smile and squeezed out the last of the mop's wetness into the sink. Done. Now to take the battle outside.

He had to leave through the front door, which was sheltered from the blast. He looked back at his handiwork before he left. The chair was holding its own against the storm, just barely. Snow was still sifting in around the edges. He'd deal with the broken door when he had tools. Right now, he had only one thing on his mind.

It was Saturday, four o'clock in the afternoon. He had been at camp almost exactly forty-eight hours, and yet here he was, standing in his *own* camp for the very first time. He had gotten here via the shutter shuttle. He had taken the six shutters he'd removed from the Hoebeeks' windows and marched them across the yard, making himself a bridge over the snow. Stepping-stones. It took him a while, and it wasn't a method of transportation that was going to get him out to the track, but all he could think about right at this very moment was what was lying before his eyes on the shelf of the little fridge on the sunporch.

Steaks.

Three T-bones. Obviously, the men had been planning on staying longer. So the biggest problem Nate really had at that precise moment was whether he was going to eat all three steaks right now or save a couple for another time. He wasn't sure how long he was going to be stuck here. He could probably do the shutter shuttle out to the work shed. There might be an old pair of snowshoes there. But that would have to wait. He was exhausted — more exhausted than he had ever been in his life, both physically and emotionally. Drained. He didn't know whether he'd be able to get out to the track by one o'clock tomorrow, but then again, the way the snow was coming down, he wasn't sure the Budd would be there, either.

He remembered times when he was younger and his father would go up for the weekend, alone, in the winter and not get home until three or four Monday morning. That was on the old timetable, when the train south was supposed to arrive at Mile 39 around four in the afternoon. His father had spent upward of eight hours waiting by the track, in the freezing cold, in the pitch-black. He'd get home with just enough time to shower and change and head off to work.

When Nate was old enough to keep up with him on snowshoes, Burl took him along. He showed him the old forty-gallon oil drum he kept in the bush off to the side of the trail out by the track. In the wintertime, it was turned upside down to keep the inside dry. And in it he kept a plastic trash bag filled with kindling, paper and dry firewood. Turn the drum upright, remove the plastic bag, and — voilà! — central heating. Then you just keep feeding it with whatever you can find.

They'd been prepared for a long wait last March: Dodge and Paul, Dad and Nate. It was a big part of the test. Surviving at camp was easy enough. Surviving the trip out was a whole other matter, since you were at the mercy of the weather and the Budd, with nowhere to hole up in. On that occasion, the Budd had come within an hour of when it was supposed to — almost a miracle. "We were lucky," Burl had said as the four of them boarded the train.

"Because I was here, Mr. Crow," said Dodge. "Mr. Lucky."

Nate didn't see the Samsung at first. Someone had left it in the fruit bowl that sat dead center on the table that took up the middle of the Crow cabin. There was no fruit in the bowl, only an assortment of flashlights and batteries, plastic bottles of Tylenol, twist tops, and such. There was an empty tub of Rolaids. Nate hoped it was Shaker who'd been having indigestion problems.

He pressed the home key of his cell phone. Nothing. But it wasn't physically broken, as far as he could see. He found his charger and plugged it in. The old AM/FM radio worked, so there was obviously enough juice stored up from the solar panels. Had Operation Drone worked? Was that why the hombres had jumped ship? He watched the phone's face, waited, and then his stomach claimed his attention and he set to work peeling potatoes and slicing up onions. A feast was in order.

The news came on the radio and he listened for anything

about escaped convicts being rounded up and taken off to some real, honest-to-God jail very far away. Nothing. The weather was big news, the last big storm of the year. They were expecting another night of it. He switched the radio off. Who knew how much power there was left; he'd better preserve it.

He boiled up the potatoes and mashed them, slathered with margarine. He fried up a can of mushrooms with onion, grilled one of the steaks, medium rare.

He hadn't eaten that entire day, so as far as he was concerned the meal he sat down to at 5:00 p.m. was breakfast. Maybe he'd eat one of the other steaks for lunch. The third for dinner . . .

Outside, the snow was cascading down, an avalanche from the heavens. Behind the veil of white, the sun was lost. It was the middle of March — spring! — and the sun wouldn't officially set until close to seven-thirty, but there wasn't a lot of light to work with. Feeling revived but sleepy at the same time, he decided he'd better find himself some snowshoes while he could — if he could. The idea of getting out to the track in time for the train Sunday now seemed possible again on a full stomach, assuming he got a good night's sleep. He suited up, put a headlamp on, and set out into the white. It was like making your way through an endless series of billowing curtains. Then when he rounded the corner of the camp, that analogy failed: it was more like a series of curtains with a heavyweight boxer behind each of them, punching invisibly at you.

He had gathered together the shutter boards and laid them out, one after the other, until he'd made it to the shed.

No snowshoes, but an old pair of his mother's cross-country skis, lying across the rafters above his head along with rakes, shovels, oars, and paddles. Some ski poles, too. He looked at the bindings on the skis. They were the old three-pronged kind. Were there any boots in the cabin that would fit them? Then again, would he be able to fit into ski boots meant for his mother? Beggars can't be choosers, he thought, and, locking up the shed, he headed back to the camp. It was dark before he closed the door — not nighttime dark, but a luminescent invisibility cloak. He closed the door on the silver-edged darkness and settled in for the night.

In a big cardboard box in the cupboard over his bed, he found an array of shoes and slippers, aqua socks, and boots of all kinds, including the ski boots meant for the three-pronged binding. Ta-da! He tried them on. Wearing winter socks, there was no way he could force his foot into the boot. With no socks on at all, he could just barely squeeze a foot in.

"Crap!"

That was not going to work. With the coming of the snow, the temperature had climbed a bit, but if he planned on trekking out to the train in these, he'd probably lose a toe or two.

So back to the drawing board.

He checked the phone again. Nothing. It had died out there, he guessed. But then why had the bad guys taken off so fast? Maybe Operation Drone had worked after all, at least in getting rid of the unwanted houseguests. They couldn't assume he *hadn't* gotten through. Whether his folks knew what was up . . . well, only time would tell. He wondered if his cell phone plan covered flying your phone in a drone and then leaving it buried in the snow overnight.

Problems for later. Meanwhile, he could breathe again. He told himself that this was all that mattered. Right now. Tried to convince himself. Tried to slough off Shaker's threat.

He stoked up the old Ashley, felt the blast of heat radiate out into the cozy room as he opened the top of the stove to lower in another piece of birch. The Ashley wasn't pretty like the shiny green Vermont Castings over at the Hoebeeks'. No windows to watch the dancing flames. But it worked gangbusters. Hah! he thought. Gangbusters.

The gang was gone. And it was going to be all right. Whether he could get out tomorrow or not, help would come eventually. He'd be down to spaghetti and rice, but he wouldn't die. As soon as he failed to show on the Budd Sunday evening, his father would be on the case. Then again, once Nate was home and safe and the world could return to something like normal, his father would be on *his* case. He had lied to him about Paul coming. He wasn't sure how much difference it would have made if Paul had been here. Couldn't say. If *Dodge* had been here, it would have made a big difference. For one thing, the Remington would have definitely come into play. They'd have all probably ended up dead.

*I'll be angry with you for the rest of your death.*

His father's words made him shudder. Dying itself didn't seem nearly so bad as having that curse hanging over your head.

He had to face the fact that he had seriously thought about using the shotgun as a last resort — thought enough to locate the two keys to unlock it as well as a box of shells. Thought enough to take it upstairs to Dodge's room with him. Thought enough to load it. And that was as far as he got. If things had gone down differently: if Shaker had come at him and the trunk didn't stop him and Cal didn't come . . . Well, it was there, the Remington, lying on the lower bunk, ready to go. Nate imagined himself backed up against the wall in the cramped little bedroom, willing the big man not to come any closer. Shuddered at the thought that he wouldn't be able to pull the trigger. Shuddered at the thought that he would.

But now, here, he was in familiar territory. No-gun territory. He stared at the books on the shelf: camp reading. He pulled down a Jack Reacher, *Worth Dying For.* Jack Reacher always found painful and satisfying ways to make the bad guys pay for their trespasses. And that's how Dodge would have wanted to play it. But would it have been worth dying for? Nate had read a couple of the books — liked them, too. Reacher was huge, a force of nature. Should have been played by Dwayne Johnson in the movies, not Tom Cruise! But tonight, the thought of the violence in the novels put him off. There had been nothing satisfying about watching Shaker fall again and again; well, okay . . . a little. But it was the kind of satisfaction that left a bad taste in your mouth. He put the book back on the shelf. He imagined some other snowy night up here, with Dad and Mom when the world was put right and all of this was ancient history. Maybe then a hard-nosed good guy beating up on some sadistic killer and his twelve closest psychotic friends would appeal to him as a good evening's entertainment. For now, it all seemed too close to home.

And if he allowed himself the luxury of relaxing, he had to think that he, Nathaniel Crow, had done a pretty good job all by himself. Done it his way.

Then he thought again of Shaker's little visit before takeoff.

*I'm going to have to mess you up so bad that your dear mama won't recognize her little boy.* Maybe he hadn't done as good a job as he could have.

# The Names of Stars

Fern Hoebeek is in the kitchen, humming along to some middle-of-the-road tune on the radio. "Oh, hi, Nate," she says, seeing him at the screen door even before he knocks.

"Is Dodge here?" he asks.

"Come on in," she says. She slaps her hands together and a cloud of flour rises before her, as if she just made something disappear. "I thought he was with you."

Nate enters the kitchen. "Nope. I slept in."

They both have the same instinct. They head into the living room to look down at the shore. Trick is making a sand castle for baby Hilton, who kicks it over as soon as Trick turns out another perfect turret. This is followed by Hilly laughing himself silly as Trick rolls around in a fit of pretend tears. Nate smiles, glad that Trick has a brother who finds him irresistible.

The motorboat is gone.

"Probably just tooling around," says Mrs. H., heading back to her dough. Nate stares at the lake. He wonders how much Mrs. H. knows about what her eldest son gets up to. He has a feeling he knows where Dodge is today. He notices out of the side of his eye the binoculars on the windowsill. He picks them up, adjusts the setting. And there's the boat, just taking off from Picnic Island. Nate puts down the binoculars. Interesting.

Dodge greets him with a head nod from twenty yards out. He's waited too long to tilt the motor to keep the prop off the bottom. Nate's stomach churns; the water gets shallow fast. He's about to yell a warning when Dodge heads to the back and leisurely tilts the motor, not a moment too soon. Nate wades out to grab the towrope and guide the boat to shore.

When they're clear of the beach and the ears of younger brothers, Nate finally speaks.

"So?"

"So what?"

"Did you do it?"

"Do what?"

"You know."

Dodge has on his *what, me?* smile, but it's a weak variant of it and it fades pretty quickly. "Yeah," he says. "I did it."

"And?"

Dodge stops and looks at him, his eyebrows pinched together as if he has detected some hint of doubt in his friend's one-word question. "I'm alive, right?" He holds his hands out to his sides, as if to say, "Look at me, I'm perfect, aren't I?"

"No prob," he says, but his eyes say different. Then he walks away, up toward the camp.

"Hey," says Nate. "Wait up."

He'd jumped. He'd jumped off the jumping cliff from the very top for the first time, or so he said. And he'd done it alone, without Nate.

"Why?" Nate asks.

"Because I didn't want your negative vibes ruining my chances," says Dodge. He stares right into Nate's eyes, daring him to challenge what he's said. There is cruelty in him, thinks Nate. He shakes away this alien thought.

Nate smiles. "You totally chickened out," he says.

Dodge's frown deepens. "Take that back," he says, quiet and deadly serious.

"You did, too," says Nate, doing a little dance. "The great D. H. chickened out."

Then Dodge is on him, his shirtfront in Dodge's fist and his face right up against Nate's. "If I said I did it, I did it. Got that?"

The smile flies from Nate's face, as if it had landed there by mistake and had business far, far away. He grabs his friend's fist and forcefully releases it from his shirt, throwing it down. Then he smooths out the front of his shirt with his palms. "Got it," he says. "And if you'd killed yourself out there without me spotting for you? What about that?"

A slow grin sneaks across Dodge's face. "If I killed myself out there, then you wouldn't have been any use anyway," he says.

Nate doesn't nod. Go find a corner and read a book, he thinks. Put some new line on your fishing rod, chop some firewood. He starts off toward his camp.

"Nate."

He turns. The smirk has gone from Dodge's face, replaced by something Nate hasn't seen much of before: fear.

"I almost hit," he says, his voice cracking a bit.

Nate walks back to him. "At the bottom?"

Dodge swallows, hard. Nods. Then glances down toward his aqua socks. The heel of his right foot is bleeding. That close.

Nate nods solemnly, aware of what Dodge just gave up — entrusted to him. The moment extends between them, full of half a lifetime of knowing each other. There is no need to say more. Nate nods again, then turns for home.

"Five at the swim raft," Dodge shouts after him, his voice cheery, as if what just happened between them was already washed clear of his memory. "Bring your Doominator," he says. "Some zombies are going to wish they'd never died!"

Nate smiles.

He woke up with the memory still turning over in his head. There was something wrong with it. Not something wrong with the memory, which was crystal clear, but with the whole thing. What? he wonders. His arms are buried under two comforters and a sleeping bag. Outside, the wind is still buffeting the camp. He's left the door open to the front room, but there's not much warmth from the woodstove. He should get up and deal with that, but for a moment he waits and thinks. He pulls his arms out from under and rests his head in the cradle of his hands on the pillow.

The boat. The Hoebeeks' boat had been pulled ashore at the picnic side of the island. That's where he'd seen Dodge leave from. So if he jumped, like he said, then how did he get back to the west side? He would have had to swim clear around the island, and that was one hell of a long swim.

Nate shook his head. He'd lied. Dodge had lied to him. He hadn't jumped. And when Nate called him on it, he had made up a story to make it seem real — so real there was even a bloody heel. He'd even dared to show signs of weakness — fear. What was most important was that Nate took him at his word. What must it be like to live like that, having to always be this person you made up?

Nate climbed out of bed and made his way into the front room, where the only light came from the cracks around the door edges of the Ashley. They'd need to buy new gaskets. He'd have to start a list. You had to keep up with the camp or it would run away on you.

It was warmer here than in his bedroom, but not much. He would feed the fire in a minute, but all he wanted to do right now was stand perfectly still and listen to the storm howling outside. He had almost given in to it. Back at the Hoebeeks' he'd almost quit on himself. Quit on everything. Allowed himself to be sucked down into the white nightmare. Now he was here in his rightful place and the wind and snow had no hold on him. He felt, for the first time since he'd arrived, a feeling of peacefulness. He sat and let it be — Nathaniel Crow alone in the eye of the storm.

He added wood to the fire, watched it catch, then closed the lid.

Awkward in the dark, he found his tattered old bathrobe, slipped it on, shoved his stocking feet into a pair of gum boots, and opened the door to the sunroom. The cabin was warm enough; the sunroom was pretty well as cold as the night. He opened the outside door — had to push hard to do it and then feel it leap from his hand when the wind caught it. *Snap!* He stepped out onto the stoop, carpeted with a smooth fleece of newly fallen snow that squeaked under his boots. He'd cleared the stoop down to the wooden deck before he went to bed, and here it was thick enough with snow that it blocked the door.

From over the eastern rim of the hill the moon glowed. He hadn't seen the moon in days. He stood in the cold, taking a pee off the stoop into fresh snow that had obliterated the yellow stains left by the men who had taken over the camp. He craned his head toward the heavens. So many stars. With his eyes half closed he carried the shine of them back to his bed.

"That one's George," says Dodge. "George Star."

"Yeah? So where's Ringo."

Dodge cuffs him. "Be serious. George is part of the constellation Ram."

"You mean like Aries?"

"No, you goof, as in the Ram truck. You see those two stars there? Those are the headlights. And that one there is the gun rack, and those two little ones are the taillights."

"Uh-huh. So who's George?"

"He's the brightest star of all, there in the cab: the driver."

Nate woke again, startled. He'd heard something. He held his breath, listened. Listened a long time before he realized that he was wrong; he'd heard the opposite of something.

# No Rest for the Wicked

The snow had stopped. It lay deep and crisp and even. The wind had stopped, too.

"Dodge?" he said. "Can you see this?"

He stood in the chilly sunroom again, squinting, looking out at the twinkling white snow on the lake. It really *did* twinkle. He hated that word; it sounded too cute, like a word that should only be used to describe the eyes of a pony in the worst kind of Saturday morning cartoon. But he didn't know another word for what was happening out there on the lake right now, half blinding him with reflected light from the sun just rising over the hills, where only a scant few hours earlier he had watched the moon sinking. The two islands stood out, dark green, as if freshly varnished, Picnic on the left, little Garbage Island on the right, the trees all decked out like a Christmas card. Twinkle, twinkle.

He raised his mug of coffee to his lips and took a slug, felt the warmth slide down into his belly. Below him, not too far beyond the invisible shoreline, the rotor wash left by the helicopter that had brought Shaker and Beck there after their escape was gone. He looked out the side window and saw the yard as pristine as the lake, with no sign that three men had made a hasty exit, roared out of here midway through yesterday afternoon. The snow had wiped away every trace of the invasion.

Good.

He headed back indoors with half a pound of bacon he'd found in the fridge and a couple of eggs, the last two in the carton. He placed them on the counter and went back to shut the door to the sunroom. But as he did, he stopped and listened, his heart in his throat. Then he laid his forehead against the cold wood of the door. A snowmobile was coming.

# Wounded

Jack Reacher would have been useful right about then. What could Nate hope to improvise against whatever was coming? The twinkling beauty of the lake in its new raiment of white — all of this had tamped down the horror show of yesterday, soothed him, turned off the survival part of his brain that could have responded to this, whatever *this* was going to be. On one hand, it could be a search-and-rescue team, with his father leading the way. At the other end of the seesaw, it could be Shaker.

Nate looked around him for a weapon. There was the poker from the fire, knives in the drawer . . . that he would never have the guts to use.

The fight had gone out of him.

"Man, you are in need of a pair!"

"Shut up, okay?"

"I'm just saying."

He shook the ghostly voice away. What he did know was that the sound was coming from the trail and not from the lake. He positioned himself at the window in his tiny bedroom, eyes glued to where the trail ended and the yard began. He'd locked the front door and the inner door that separated the living area from the sleeping quarters. He'd brought with him his weapon of choice: a pot that had been sitting on top of the stove, full of near boiling water. He wasn't going to win any battle requiring brute strength, not with the likes of Shaker. Surprise was all he had to work with. As the sled got closer, he wondered if Shaker would go to the Hoebeeks' first, assuming Nate was there. Then the noise got really loud and his question was answered. Any second now he'd appear. . . .

But it wasn't Shaker.

Carrying the pot back to the kitchen, Nate checked out the side window to where Cal Crow had brought his snowmobile to a stop within a couple steps of the stoop. Nate watched him try to stand on the runners, leaning hard on the handlebars for support. He turned slowly, stepped down into the depth of snow, and just stood there, as if he'd stepped into a vat of cement. His left leg appeared damp, the fabric of his snowsuit torn — punctured — halfway down his inner thigh.

Nate raced to the door, plunged his feet back into his gum boots, and tore out to the stoop. He'd left the shutters from the Hoebeeks' place against the wall beside the back door. Now he took one of the larger ones and laid it down across the snow.

Cal looked at him, saw what he was doing. He tore off his ski mask and shoved it in his pocket, nodded toward the plywood board, but still couldn't move. Nate stepped out onto the shutter.

"Just fall forward," said Nate. "I'll get you." And without a word, Cal did as he was told. He fell and the upper part of his body landed on the plywood, which he grappled with the way a swimmer shimmies his way onto a raft. Nate tried to help but the old man growled at him — or at the pain he was obviously in. As soon as he was aboard, he rose to his knees — his right knee, at least — and crawled, dragging his left leg toward the stoop, where Nate helped him to his feet, took him under his shoulder, and helped him inside.

"Leave me alone!" the old man said, swatting at him, but Nate had an end goal in sight; he'd already pushed the table out of the way and dragged the largest of the armchairs over near the woodstove. Fending off the swats and curses, he finally was able to dump Cal down into the chair.

"Jeezus H. Christ!" Cal shouted. "You damn near kilt me!"

He leaned back breathing hard. He wrestled the zipper of his parka down with what must have been his last bit of energy, because the next thing Nate knew the man was sitting completely still, his dark head against the head rest, the muscles on his scrawny neck standing out like cables. Nate stood a couple of paces away, catching his breath, watching the pain animate his grandfather's face. His arms lay at rest on the arms of the chair, his fists curled not quite tight. Nate watched, waiting for him to succumb — to just die, right there. When he didn't, Nate mobilized again and headed toward the back room.

"Where the hell you goin'?" the man shouted.

"There's a first-aid kit," said Nate.

"Don't first-aid me. I'll tell ya what I need. But I can just bet your damn father don't hold with alcohol."

Nate stood over by the door to the sleeping section, not sure what to do. Maybe take one of the cast-iron frying pans he'd been about to use and put the old coot out of his misery. Instead, he turned to the open cupboards that lined the north wall to the left of the doorway into the bedrooms. He pushed aside some cans and canisters until he found what he was after.

"Here," he said.

Cal didn't open his eyes right off. Then he did — one of them — and tried to focus on what Nate was holding. A bottle about a quarter full of Johnnie Walker.

"The Lord be praised," Cal muttered, and reached out with a feeble hand for the booze. Nate unscrewed the top for him. He handed him a glass, which Cal waved away. Then Nate went to the back room. He checked the window first, opened it to see if he could hear another sled approaching. No. He shut the window and grabbed the first-aid kit.

Cal tried to wave him off again, but he seemed distracted enough by the whisky to let Nate kneel in front of him and try to get a look at what was under the bloody hole in the overalls.

"You're going to need to get out of them," he said.

Cal told him to screw off. Nate waited. The old man took another swig of the whisky, his hand so shaky that a trickle escaped down the side of his unshaven chin.

"I could cut them off," said Nate.

"I'll cut you off, boy."

"Okay," said Nate, and got to his feet. "I think I'm going to go change."

He was gone less than five minutes, but when he returned the man was asleep. The bottle was empty, though he still held it by the neck, cradled in his lap. Nate could see fresh blood seeping from the wound on his leg, but there was nothing he could do. He went to the window, looked out at the snowmobile. He hadn't noticed at first that it was his father's Ski-Doo. When Cal arrived two days ago, he had been on a different sled, a big Sidewinder. What had happened? There were a lot of unanswered questions, some of them more pressing than others. Like how far were Shaker and Beck behind him? Who shot him? And if it was Shaker, did he have his eyes on Nate for his next victim? He was pretty sure it was a gunshot wound. In his mind's eye, he could see that weapon Shaker had been waving around yesterday, and something told him that it wouldn't have been too long before it went off.

"You still here?"

Nate walked over to the old man and looked down at him. "How you feeling?"

"Like I don't plan on dancin' tonight," said Cal.

"Are they coming back?"

Cal made a sour face. "Beck, not likely. On account of being dead . . . well, maybe." He shook his head. "I dunno. Sure made a lot of noise when he went down."

"And the other guy?"

"Shaker?" Cal waved at the air. "He hied off who knows where." He sniffed. "You got any more of this here medicine?"

Nate hesitated, then shook his head.

"Yeah, you do, boy," said Cal. He hadn't missed the fractional moment of indecision. "Now you go get it for your old granddaddy."

There was an unopened bottle of whisky tucked away. His father didn't drink much, a beer or two on a hot day. But they always had something on hand in case company dropped by. Art Hoebeek liked a snoot full, as he put it.

"Ya hear me, boy?"

"I'll make you a deal," said Nate.

"Hah! You think this is some kinda game show?"

"No wonder Dad never had you around for Sunday dinner," said Nate. Cal sneered. No wonder Burl never even mentioned his name. The man was just plain foul. Still, for some reason, Nate found it all weirdly amusing. "Two things," he said.

That got Cal's attention. He stared at Nate through eyes that looked like they hadn't gotten much sleep last night. "Two things?" he said.

Nate held up his hand with two fingers extended. "Two things," he repeated.

The old man couldn't seem to quite believe what was happening, judging from the surprise on his face. He tried to knock Nate over with his eyes. Failed. Tried to reach out and grab him, but the Johnnie Walker had made him slow and Nate easily stepped back out of reach. Finally, the old man spoke again. "Okay, shoot."

"First," said Nate, "you call me by my name."

"Oh, f—"

"It's Nate, in case you forgot. I'm not 'boy' or 'kid.' You want something, you ask nicely."

If his wound wasn't about to kill the old man, Nate's demand seemed like it might. He swore some, mostly under his breath.

"Okay, *Nate*," he finally said. "And . . . ?"

"And second, you get out of those pants."

"What the—"

"So I can see what's going on with your leg."

The swearing this time was riper, and if God was at work today — it being Sunday — he got an earful, a fair bit of it aimed his way, but not exclusively; both of Nate's parents fared pretty badly in Cal's assessment of the work they'd been doing bringing up their son. But finally he ran out of steam. He closed his eyes. His breath was ragged. He was fighting hard. He opened one eye.

"Ya still here?" he said. "I was havin' this nightmare. . . ."

Nate didn't bother to answer. The amusement value was running low. And he didn't like the idea that Shaker was still at large.

He must have gotten something across with the bitter expression on his face, because the old man reached up and undid the top of his bib and then, with a lot of pain and the language to go with it, stripped off his overalls until they puddled at his feet. Nate grimaced at the sight of the old man's boxers. Wondered what decade he'd last changed them.

The exertion needed to strip down helped to knock some of the noise out of Cal. He leaned back in the chair again, looking vulnerable, looking spent. And with his skinny legs exposed, he suddenly looked very, very old. Nate focused on the wound. It was on the inside of his left thigh, about halfway between crotch and knobby knee. Any thought that the wound was made by anything other than a bullet disappeared as soon as Nate laid eyes on it. The perforation of the skin was perfectly round, exposing the raw red of muscle. He couldn't see a bullet. Gently, he moved the leg inward and peered at the outer side of Cal's thigh. No sign of an exit wound. So the bullet was in there. But there was no way he was going in with tweezers. It was still oozing, the heart pumping blood to the site.

"I'm going to have to raise your leg," he said.

When Cal didn't answer, Nate glanced at his face. The old man simply nodded. Nate got a couple of pillows and draped a couple of towels over them on a kitchen chair. Cal cried out when Nate lifted the leg, but he was too weak to shake the boy off, and soon enough Nate had Cal's wounded limb up higher than his heart. It didn't seem like it would be enough. In his parents' room, he found an old worn belt of his dad's. When he got back, his patient's eyes were closed. Good. Carefully, he wrapped the belt around Cal's upper thigh, cinched it, and then slowly tightened it. He didn't get far before the old man exploded with pain, swatting at Nate and hurling every expletive Nate had ever heard and some new ones, too. Then he fell back against the chair, spent, and after a moment drifted off again.

Okay, thought Nate. So much for a tourniquet.

Which is when he noticed the burn marks. He'd been concentrating on the new wound, livid and bright as an angry bull's eye. Now he saw the curdled skin that marked pretty much the entire outer side of the man's other leg. The hair growth was patchy; there were some areas that were yellow, with a texture like parchment. Nate could see similar marks on the left leg as well. Fire damage. As little as he knew about this man, he knew where he got these wounds. Same place his dad did. On this very spot: the camp that used to sit right here before Cal burned it to the ground. His eyes traveled to the man's face. He was awake again, observing Nate, but his lips were clamped tightly shut. This wasn't a time for a chat. Nate snapped his attention back to the bullet wound.

Elevating the leg seemed to have slowed down the hemorrhaging a little, or maybe that was just wishful thinking. He felt Cal's foot. It was cool, even near the fire. He looked around; the old man was watching him with one beady eye. "Wiggle your toes," said Nate. Cal wiggled his toes. Nate nodded. "Good. You've still got some sensation down there."

"You're gonna get some sensation you try wrappin' a belt 'round me again."

Nate stared at him. "You want to die? That can be arranged."

Cal almost smiled. "Get on with it," he said.

Nate nodded. He needed to wash out the wound. He didn't think this was going to go over too well.

"This is going to sting," he said, and didn't wait for Cal's response as he poured hydrogen peroxide over the wound. Cal flinched, but this time held his tongue. Then Nate tore open with his teeth an antiseptic wipe and patted down the area around the bullet hole. There was antibiotic ointment in the kit as well; that came next, and then, as rapidly as he could make it happen, two absorbent compresses, with adhesive tape to hold them in place. Finally, a four-inch-wide roller bandage wrapped as tightly as Nate dared around the thigh, without cutting off circulation.

He stared at the job, leaning back on his haunches.

"You study first aid?" said Cal, his voice modulated and calmer now. Nate nodded. "Your daddy make you do that?" Nate looked at him warily. He nodded again.

"Yeah," said Cal, closing his eyes. "'Spected as much." Even in his injured state, he managed to imbue those few words with scorn.

Nate cleared up the mess on the floor as best as he could. Cal had gone quiet. The bullet was in there; who knew what damage it was causing. But there was nothing else Nate could do. He turned away, opened the top of the Ashley, and threw in whatever of the trash would burn.

"What about your part of the bargain?" said Cal.

Nate turned. "What's that?"

Cal managed a tight little smile as he tilted his hand, thumb up, toward his open mouth. "Glug, glug, glug."

"Oh, right," Nate said, and went to find the unopened bottle of scotch.

# The Ambush

"What happened?"

Nate sat staring at Cal, who was awake again after having drifted off for half an hour. He glanced at Nate and then his eyes strayed to the glass on the wide, flat arm of the chair. Nate had only given him a glass of scotch from the new bottle, afraid he might drink the whole thing, and then where would they be? Cal's gaze lifted to Nate hopefully, but Nate showed no sign of interpreting the look Cal was giving him. And so Cal began.

"Ambush."

"An ambush?"

"That's what I said. Cops."

"Whoa! Maybe you'd better start at the beginning."

The escaped convicts had followed Cal Crow to the Branigan logging camp. There was no one there to meet them. The place was closed down, locked up. They broke in and waited.

"You know how well Shaker takes to waitin'," said Cal. He shook his head. "I shoulda guessed somethin' was up. Shoulda been able to tell from the way Beck was actin'. Kept apologizin' for how long it was takin'. 'Well, what'd you expect?' he'd say. 'I mean, it's only a few hours since I talked to them,' and blah, blah, blah." Cal frowned. "It's always the one who talks too much got something bad hid up his sleeve." He shook his head. "At first, I figured he was on edge because Shaker was working himself into one of his frenzies, pacing back and forth, wearing out the floorboards, building up a real head of steam. He's a mean bugger behind all his fancy language. When he's on edge, anybody in their right mind oughta be on edge. That's what I was thinkin'."

"Who was supposed to be coming?"

"The mob. The boys are well connected, if you know what I mean."

"You mean like gangsters? The Mafia?"

"Yeah, sure. Whatever. The folks in these parts who run the gambling operations, loan sharkin', extortion, drugs — you name it. Gangbangers."

"Oh. Right."

"The ones broke the lads out of jail. Like I said, well connected. Beck is a hustler. They're a dime a dozen. It wasn't him they wanted. Shaker, on the other hand, is valuable to those folks. He'll do people for you. That's what he was in for."

"You mean kill people?"

Cal nodded. Raised his hand, index finger out like a gun barrel. "Bang!" he said.

It wasn't anything Nate really wanted to hear. "A hit man," he said.

Cal nodded. "Probably more than a few, but they was only ever able to pin one on him that stuck. Some scuzzbag whose leaving the earth has made it a better place. Thing is, it's still a capital offense. Don't you just love democracy?" Cal wagged his head with disgust, and Nate wondered at how Cal could manage to have ideals about wrong and right. "Anyway, the mob wanted Shaker back; he's as crazy as a rat in a garbage can, but, like I said, he's useful. And Beck . . . Well, he happened to be in the same jail, so it was a twofer."

"A twofer . . ."

Cal's eyes rolled. "Two for one."

"Right." Nate was struggling to keep up. "So the ambush . . ."

"Didn't see it comin'," said Cal. He tried to move, make himself more comfortable, but ended up groaning in agony at the attempt. "Christ, what'd you do to me?" he shouted.

"While you were sleeping, I shoved a bullet into this handy hole in your leg," said Nate.

Cal burned a hole in Nate's forehead with his eyes but didn't comment. Then his face contorted with pain again and Nate made an executive decision. He went back to the shelf and got the bottle of Johnnie Walker. He poured Cal a couple of fingers' worth.

"That's more like it. And just leave the bottle, why don't you."

But Nate put it out of reach on the table, and was cursed for his efforts. Then he straddled the kitchen chair just out of reach of the old man. "The ambush," he said.

Cal took a swig and swished the alcohol around in his mouth as if it were mouthwash. He swallowed, winced, sighed, wiped his dry lips with the back of his forearm. "Kev's plan, hah! It wasn't Kev Beck was talkin' to at all. He was gettin' cozy with the pigs instead, hopin' to make some kind of a plea bargain, I guess. I don't know. I don't know why I ever got involved with those two lunatics."

"So why did you?"

"I just tol' ya!" said Cal. "I don't friggin' know!" Then he lowered his voice. "They was in the slammer, waiting to be sent south. I was in there serving a short sentence. And don't ask me what for; the pigs don't need a damn reason to throw your ass in jail once you're on their watch list." He fumed for a minute and Nate studied his face, half shocked and half fascinated that this man could share the slightest bit of DNA with his father — or himself. "I seen them there, Beck and Shaker. I knew who they was. Not by name. Di'n't *know* them; just knew they was connected. Con-neck-ted." His tired, wet eyes lit up for a moment. "I seen 'em in the lunchroom talkin' 'cross the table, quiet, by themselves. No one went near 'em. But I could tell they was cookin' somethin' up. I got an eye for that." He looked at Nate, and perhaps he was hoping for the boy to be impressed because he snarled when Nate didn't react.

"If I was ever going to make some serious dough, I needed to get in with these people. And so I takes a chance. I jus' walk up to 'em at lunch and sit down right there beside 'em, interrupt their little chin-wag." He paused, shook his head. "I start right in. 'Gen'lemen. Be glad you're eatin' in this pigsty 'stead of the staff room.'" He managed a tight little smile. "They just stared at me. 'Yep,' I said. 'I mean the whole place is a pigsty, but that lunchroom . . .'" He took another swig, his eyes staring off into the warm air over the Ashley. "The staff room has this hollow sound to it. The room is kind of echoey. You know why?" Nate wasn't sure if this was part of his remembered conversation or whether Cal was talking to him. He shook his head. "Because it's where the drop was, Nathaniel." Cal's eyes were large with meaning, a meaning Nate couldn't grasp.

"I don't understand."

"That's where they hung people, back in the day."

"Oh."

"You can still see where the trapdoor was on the staff room floor. Below that is this pit where the body would fall." He shook his head. "The body would drop down to right outside the laundry room in the basement, where the tunnel is to the courthouse."

"Really?"

Cal nodded. "That's exactly what Beck said. 'Really?' Meanwhile, Shaker's staring a hole in his sandwich. Then he looks at me. 'And how would you know such things?' he asks. And I say, 'I seen it.' And he says, 'When you were having a bite with your good friends the guards? A narc, maybe? Some kind of snitch?'"

Cal shook his head and looked up at Nate. "I figure I'm this close to him putting a fist through my head, so I quicken things up. 'Nothin' like that,' I said. 'I was just mopping the floors, is all.' Then before Shaker can ask any more questions, I lean in close and come right out with it. 'Gen'lemen,' I said, 'if you're plannin' a break, maybe you need a plan B.'"

Cal trained his eyes on Nate, and despite everything, Nate was hooked. "A plan B?"

"You got 'er."

"You said that?"

"Not those exact words. But the thing is, they *was* plannin' a break. And they *did* need a plan B —'cept maybe they didn't know that right off, like. Took 'em a bit to come around. And since I was gonna be on the outside in just a few days, it all just come together."

"So why did they need a plan B?"

Cal seemed to be warming to the story. And strangely, Nate recognized the pattern. It was kind of like Dodge. Dodge was never as happy as when he was talking about some caper he'd pulled off, or some unsuspecting goof at school he'd played for a sucker.

So Cal talked about how the mob had their fingers in all sorts of pies, including a lot of stock in a major construction company in Sudbury, a company with its own helicopter. The thing was to make it anonymous, so they spray-painted over all the distinguishing markers on it. But that was only ever going to be a stopgap, and they knew it. There weren't a whole lot of Robinson R22 choppers in the area, so soon enough the cops would be around to check on the company helicopter, which would have been washed clean by then. Time was the big factor. How soon would the cops have roadblocks up, and how extensive would they be? How soon could they get the guys to some safe house and return the helicopter to home base? Shaker was considered a dangerous offender, about to serve a life sentence for murder. They got those roadblocks up real fast.

"Which is where I come in," said Cal. "I could provide these guys with a place right off the map. Not more than a hop, skip, and a jump from the jail in a copter that can go one hundred and seventy miles an hour and fly under the radar. The copter could be back at the construction yard in two or three hours, max, and the boys could cool their heels until things settled down.

"*And*," said Cal, "I know how to get out of this place by pathways very few people knows about." He chuckled darkly. "That's where Shaker and Beck got it all wrong, cooking up with Kev — whoever the hell he is — some way to squeeze me out of the picture and out of the money we settled on."

Nate watched the story play out on Cal's torn-up face. Saw him turn in his thin lower lip and bite down hard on it as another jolt of pain disturbed the memory of how smart he'd been to horn in on the escape plans and deliver on his promise. Then Nate watched the pain win out over the pride, saw the whole stupid escapade dissolve in the old man's eyes. He seemed to suddenly become aware of Nate looking at him, and fixed his gaze on him. "What are you gawkin' at?" he snapped.

"Nothing," said Nate. Then he got out of his chair and tended to the hungry woodstove. By the time he returned his attention to his grandfather, there wasn't a shred of satisfaction left in his expression.

"I'm an old fool," he said, his voice reduced to a smoker's grumble. "I di'n't see that ambush coming. Di'n't know I was being bushwhacked, until *you* told me. You, of all people, for God's sake." He shook his head.

"But you got away," said Nate. "That's something."

"Somethin', yeah. But I'm not gettin' nothin' else out of it — not one goddamned nickel — just a bullet in the leg."

Nate waited before he spoke again, waited for the bitter expression on Cal's face to pass. "So the cops shot Beck and —"

"Hell, no. Shaker did that! Soon as he figured what was goin' on."

"And then he took off?"

Cal nodded. "The cops didn't get nobody. Completely blew it. Well, they got Beck, all right, but it was Shaker they wanted."

"And he —"

"Took off, like I told ya. I didn't see it. Just heard him shoot Beck, heard Beck caterwauling. I'd already left the premises. Shaker shot me when I was hightailin' it outa there." He sighed with exasperation, took another swig of his whisky.

Nate looked at the wound on the man's inner thigh. "How'd he get you *there*?" he said.

Cal looked down. "Ricochet, I guess. That old wreck of a Ski-Doo's got itself a nasty little dent." He smiled. "Your daddy's sure gonna like that, eh?" Nate didn't bother to reply. And Cal didn't look as if he were truly worried about the destruction of other people's property. His expression was one of outrage. "As if *I* was in on the double cross, for God's sake. Hell, all I wanted was my pay. I wanted some real mazuma for a change — enough to get the hell out of here for once and for all. I sure didn't want this!" He smacked his leg and immediately regretted it.

Meanwhile, Nate was on his feet, though he couldn't move, seemed glued to the floor. "So where is he? Shaker, I mean."

Cal held up his hand. "I was getting to that. Just hold your horses, kid. Sit down."

Nate did not obey. He crossed his arms on his chest. He'd had enough storytelling. Self-aggrandizing storytelling. God, Cal *was* like Dodge.

"I got out," said Cal. "Saw the writin' on the wall quicker 'n Shaker did. Said I was steppin' out the back to take a piss and skedaddled. I took a shot for it, but it could have been worse." He managed a dry cough of a laugh. "He let off a bunch of rounds in my direction. Not sure how he ever got to be a hit man with such lousy aim. Anyway, I stopped on a ridge above the loggin' camp to figure out what was going on. I could see a bunch of vehicles followin' a grader in. A grader, for Christ's sake! I don't exactly know how Beck planned on explainin' where the mob got its hands on a municipal grader. Meanwhile, Shaker took off in the other direction, south. I guess it looked like the best direction to go to put as much space between him and the boys in blue."

"So not this way, then?" said Nate.

Cal shook his head. Then he patted the air with his hand, attempting to get Nate to sit down. Nate didn't. "Where was he heading?"

"Nowhere," said Cal. "Away. That's all he could think of. Get outa there while the gettin's good."

Nate tried to relax but the thought of that man on the loose wouldn't let him.

Cal downed the last of his drink and placed the glass firmly on the arm of his easy chair. "Here's the thing," he said. "With any luck, he followed a loggin' trail out to hell and gone, where he's gonna run out of gas and end up where he belongs, a few rungs down on the food chain. If that happens and if they find him at all, there won't be more than a few well-gnawed bones. That's one scenario."

Nate liked that scenario. What he didn't like was the idea that there might be another. "But . . ." was all he could make himself say.

"But if he comes to his senses — and I'm not sure whether he's got any — he might just try heading back."

"Why?" said Nate. "I mean, if the cops are around."

"The cops may be around, dependin' on how long it takes them to get their act together. Whoever Beck talked to about the ambush wasn't a whole lot aware of what he was heading into. So there was nobody chasin' nobody — not right away. They didn't chase me, that's for sure, but then I was out of there lickety-split. And they wouldn't have been able to take off after Shaker, neither. They'd need to radio back to headquarters and get some equipment together." He shook his head, marveling at the lunacy of the operation. "Morons," he said.

At last, Nate sat down. "So I guess things are okay," he said.

"Ya think?"

The look on Cal's face was not reassuring. "What?" said Nate.

"If that big lunk is smart — and that's a big if — then he's gonna wanna double back this way sooner or later because one, he's gonna need fuel, and two, he's gonna need somethin' a whole lot more important than that."

Nate stared at Cal, who stared right back at him. "What do you mean?"

Cal fixed him with a dark eye. "A hostage," he said.

# Wait. It. Out.

The first order of business was to get the Ski-Doo fueled up. Cal said he had a plan. He wouldn't say what, not yet, and Nate wasn't really sure he had a plan at all, but he was glad to be doing something, anything. He hopped on the sled and started her up. She purred. Not a big purr — not a growl worthy of a big cat — but the contented purr of a fat old tom well looked after. Nate revved the motor; he knew this machine pretty well. He swung it around the bright-white expanse of the yard a couple times, liking the feel of the wind in his face after being cooped up inside so long. Liked the cleanness of the air after the stink of injury. Then he slewed over to the shed in back of the cabin where they kept the Kawasaki ATV and, in a room off it, all the various blends of fuel they used for the outboard motor, the pump, the chain saw, the lawn mower, et cetera. There were extra propane cylinders there as well. Good to know, as far as keeping the oven working if he was going to be stuck here any length of time.

There was a shovel hanging on the outside wall of the shed. The invaders had dug out the doors to get the auger, and for the first time on this whole ill-fated trip, the wind seemed to have actually done Nate a favor: the new snowfall wasn't as thick in front of the shed doors as he might have expected. He made short work of it, energized at the thought of getting away. Right now, getting away seemed the most desirable alternative. Without his phone, he wasn't sure what time it was, but it was still early enough to catch the Budd. That's what he wanted more than anything, and now he had a means of getting out to the track. He unlocked the door, opened it just enough to squeeze through.

Hell, he could go *now!*

Just fuel up and leave the old man where he was. Cal was bandaged and warm and God knows he seemed feisty enough. He could probably drag himself to the fridge for some food. After all, he'd been living in the place for days, seemed to use it whenever he felt like it! Nate was suddenly seized by rage. That old man in there was the architect of everything that had gone wrong. He was the one who'd brought these criminals to the camp — one of them a murderer!

Just leave him! Get out to the Budd, and when you're safe onboard, ask the conductor to radio medevac. And the police while you're at it.

Split. Get out of here. Let people who know what they're doing do what they're paid to do.

He stood there, his hot breath blooming into frozen vapor in front of his face. "That's the spirit, Numbster," said a familiar voice in his head. "Let the old bastard cool his heels — literally!"

"Calm down," said the voice of his father.

No, Dad, Dodge is right. Doesn't this all sound way too famil-iar? Didn't Cal almost get you killed, too? That's what he wanted to say to Burl. And in his mind, his father nodded but didn't say anything else. Nate stood there in the dimness of the shed with its fumes and the hardness and smell of frozen earth below his feet. "Hear him out," his father said. "You don't need to obey him. You don't owe him that."

This is *my* place, Nate thought. And the father in his head was silent but nodded knowingly, agreeing with him. After all, Nate had passed the test. "I can look out for myself," said Nate, out loud this time. And the father in him said, "You can. But can you look out for the likes of someone like Shaker?"

Nate screwed the top on the gasoline can extra tight after he'd finished with it and put it back where it was stored, nice and neat. He locked the shed door.

The next thing on Cal's to-do list he felt even more uncer-tain about. He powered the snowmobile through the break of trees that separated the Crow camp from the Hoebeeks' place and around to the front deck. He entered through the door, which he'd left unlocked. The camp had cooled down again. It felt strange to be here, even with the light pouring in — maybe especially because of the light. It had been the scene of so many good times: wild board games on rainy days, a hundred noisy lunchtimes. And now it was also the site of the most harrowing twenty-four hours of his life. He looked at the back door barricaded by the old chair. Snow, with the help of the bully wind, had made a forced entrance, if only around the edges, and lay gathered in low drifts at the feet of the chair. Nate's boots echoed as he made his way to the master bedroom, to the closet, but the Remington wasn't there. Then he remembered. He'd taken it upstairs, which was where he found it, lying on the bunk, loaded and ready to go. He grabbed a box of shells as he was leaving. He had a very bad feeling about this.

"An 870," said Cal, taking the gun from him. He was still in his chair by the fire. He looked the gun over, saw the trigger lock. "What's the combination?" he said. Nate swallowed hard. Cal looked up at him and his dark eyebrows knitted together. "Oh, for Christ's sake boy, don't get all gummy-brained on me now."

"I don't want you firing this thing in the camp."

"Well, let's hope it don't come to that. But we gotta be ready for the worst."

It made sense, being ready for the worst. That's why Art Hoebeek had bought the gun in the first place. But Burl had not been pleased about it. Nate could remember the look on his father's face. "Why is it," he'd said, "that planning for the worst is the most likely way to ensure it happens?" But it wasn't Burl's place to say what Art Hoebeek did or didn't do, although he did convince his neighbor to get the trigger lock.

"Boy? You still with us?"

He looked at Cal, who was waiting on him, waiting for an answer, with nothing approaching patience on his face.

"The name's Nate. Remember? And I don't want to be cleaning up any blood."

"Good point," said Cal, nodding. "And the beauty of it is that if Shaker decides to go on one of his rampages, you won't be around to have to clean up nothin'."

Reluctantly, Nate agreed, but when he tried to take the gun from Cal, the old man held on to it. "Just give me the numbers," he said.

"No," said Nate.

"Kid, I'm —"

"No!" said Nate. "If I do, then it's just one more thing you can get your hands on whenever you feel like coming up here and . . . I don't know . . . pretending like you own the place."

Cal's body went rigid and his eyes steely. Nate stepped back, out of the range of the man's anger. "Didn't anybody teach you to respect your elders?"

"Yeah," said Nate. "But not criminals. Not people who break into your camp."

"If I wanted to, I could teach you a lesson right now, gimpy leg or not, that you'd never forget."

"Like you did my father? That kind of lesson?"

Cal held his eyes in a tug-of-war gaze. But it wasn't any game to Cal; he wasn't used to being crossed. And Nate wasn't used to anyone talking to him like this. He would not give in. Not here, of all places. He reminded himself that if push came to shove, all he needed to do was whack the old man in the thigh. The thought of it was just enough to keep him strong and determined.

Cal blinked first. Nate saw him release the stranglehold on the gun, useless without what Nate was keeping from him. Then he handed the gun to him with the ill grace of a five-year-old having to give back a toy to his baby brother. Nate moved away so Cal couldn't see the numbers he was inputting. Seven-zero-eight. The month and year the Hoebeeks moved to Ghost Lake. He put the trigger lock on the table and handed Cal the gun. He swiped it from Nate's hands.

"You'll be thankin' me, boy, when I save your sorry ass."

Nate's heart was beating like a drum. Don't say anything, he told himself. Just don't bother. This man might be his grandfather, but Nate meant nothing to him. He'd already forgotten their bargain and Nate was back to being just "you" or "kid" or "boy."

Cal pulled back the pump and checked the chamber, felt

inside with his finger to see if it was empty. Nate already knew it was. Cal closed the chamber, lay the Remington across the arms of his chair. "Ammo," he said. Nate patted the pocket of his parka. Cal sneered. "It's not gonna do much good in there," he said.

"There's going to be lots of warning when and if Shaker comes back. I'll give you the ammo then."

It was just about the last straw for Cal. Without taking his eyes off Nate, he lifted his bad leg from the chair piled with pillows and planted it on the floor. "I can still whup you, you know. It'd take more than a scratch to keep me from putting you on your back."

Nate stared at him. *I can still whup you.* Suddenly he realized why the old man couldn't call him by his name: he didn't see him as Nate. He saw him as Burl, as the boy he'd beat on, sent running off, sent into the wilderness, because it was here — right here — that Burl had ended up when he finally escaped from the old man's fists. And knowing that, Nate felt his backbone straighten.

*He thinks I'm Burl.*

Without knowing it, Cal Crow had done exactly the wrong thing if he hoped to intimidate him.

Cal was leaning forward in his chair. He had laid the gun aside. His hands, fingers splayed, were on the arms of the chair, ready to push himself up, his eyes full of threat. And instead of backing farther away, Nate came to him.

"Maybe this stuff worked on my dad, but I wasn't brought up with it. You don't frighten me."

It was as if he had spoken to Cal in a foreign language. The simmering rage in the man was doused by incomprehension. "What'd you say to me?"

Nate just shook his head. He wasn't going to play this game. And he knew something now — knew it beyond the shadow of a doubt: this is what made his father hold his words, keep to the strength of silence. Wait.

Wait. It. Out.

Cal lowered himself back down into the chair. His face contorted, as if anger had suppressed, momentarily, the pain he was in. He leaned back, breathing heavily. Nate waited another moment and then slowly approached him. He squatted down beside the man's wounded leg and then gently raised it to lay the foot again on the chair with the cushions so that the wound was above Cal's heart.

# The Plan

Cal swatted at his eyes. They were wet — whether with pain or grief, Nate was not about to ask. "He di'n't always hate me, ya know."

"Pardon?"

"Your father. We got along okay for a bit there. When he was a kid." Nate's shoulders went slack. There was bitterness in the downward curve of his grandfather's mouth. He looked at Nate. His breathing was shallow. "He ever tell ya about his sister?"

Nate tried to think. He had no aunt on his father's side of the family. Not one he knew about. Wait, yes. Now he remembered. There had been a sister, but she died. He didn't remember anything more about it. He nodded vaguely.

If Cal had been going to say more, the expression on Nate's face must have changed his mind. He blinked a couple of times, as if returning from somewhere a long way off. Then he stared at the woodstove.

What was there to say to such a man? Actually, Nate knew exactly what he wanted to say. He again straddled the nearby chair, resting his chin on the top of it.

"What's your plan?"

The old man seemed surprised, suspicious, as if Nate had pulled the rug out from under him. Disarmed him. He glanced at him, disoriented. Maybe there was no plan after all. He waited.

"Okay," said Cal. "Except, I don't think you're gonna like it."

"Most likely. Try me."

"You're going to set this here chair up, right over there, facing the front door." He turned to look at the door. "'Bout five feet back, I'd say." He sniffed, rubbed his nose. "Yeah, that oughta do it. Then, once you give me that box of shells, you're gonna make me a sandwich or two, give me back that bottle of Johnnie Walker Red you've been hoarding, and leave. Beat it."

Nate stared at him. "That's all? That's your plan?"

"If that big bruiser comes through the door with a gun in his hand, I'm gonna need some method of persuadin' him to put it down. After all, I wouldn't want to get your nice clean linoleum all covered with gore or nothin'."

Nate frowned. "I don't have any idea what time it is. Are you saying I just head out to the track and leave you here?"

"Don't say you di'n't think about it," said Cal. "You out there in the shed toppin' up the Ski-Doo. Sure you did. Get the hell outa here, you was thinkin'."

"Maybe I was."

"No maybe about it."

"But the thing is, I didn't go."

"Well, there's still time." He swiveled his head around to squint out the window at the sun. "By my calculations, it's before noon.

You oughta have enough time to rendezvous with the train if you head out right away."

Nate sat up straight, his frown deepening. "If I take the Ski-Doo, I can be out at the track in fifteen, twenty minutes, max. And there's no way it's going to be on time anyway."

Cal held up his finger. "Ah, that's where you got it wrong. You think I'm talking about Mile Thirty-Nine."

"What do you mean? I should head down the lake, catch it at Southend?" Cal nodded. "But why?"

"Because, you damn fool, if Shaker *is* able to find his way back here, he'll be comin' down that same damn trail and you'd never be able to turn around, even if you heard him, which you wouldn't anyhow because you'd be makin' as much racket as he was."

Nate hadn't really thought of that. He wasn't used to thinking of the trail as two-lane, let alone dangerous. He shook his head, more out of bewilderment than anything else.

"You don't believe me?"

"It's not that," said Nate. "I mean . . . Okay, he takes off from this logging camp, running from the cops. If he weren't here by now, then he must have found some other way out or, like you said, run out of fuel."

"Could be," said Cal. "And like I said before, that'd be the best a man or boy could wish for. But there are other camps. More'n one camper uses them loggin' roads, and this time of year it's easy as hell to find one: just follow the guy's trail in the snow. That sadistic lunatic — he ain't gonna have any problem coaxing some fool out of his fuel. Or a place to stay for the night, with his host hog-tied or chucked out in the cold. Hell, he might steal himself a whole new snowmobile."

Nate hadn't thought of that, either. He wasn't in the habit of thinking like a criminal. But the whole thing bothered him, and he wasn't quite sure why. "So you were saying earlier that he'd come back here because he needs a hostage. If he finds somebody out there and he's planning on stealing their snowmobile anyway, why wouldn't he just make them his hostage? Why would he want to come all the way back here and take the risk of running into the cops on the way?"

Now Cal grinned, every trace of confusion gone. He leaned forward in his chair. "Because he's got a hate on for you, Nathaniel Crow. Ain't that the truth?" Reluctantly, Nate nodded. "And you gotta understand somethin': that SOB would travel a thousand miles to make life miserable for someone who crossed him."

Nate believed it. Shaker might want to keep him alive as a bargaining chip, but that didn't mean he wouldn't make things hard on him. Still, the plan didn't sit right with him. He looked at Cal. "What about you?"

"What about me? I got food, a bottle, and a twelve-gauge. Sounds like a party to me."

"But —"

"Shut it!" said Cal. He picked up the gun and held the butt end up threateningly. "You want butt, I'll give you butt."

Nate sighed and raised his hands in surrender. This man had no knack for conversation. Everything was a show of force — retaliation. But Nate was the one who was mobile and the one who had the ammo for that Remington.

"If I'm heading down the lake, why don't you come, too?"

"Yeah, right. I'm gonna ride tandem with this leg? No, thank you."

"We've got a new freight sled."

"You gotta be kidding me."

"I'm not. I can fill it up with, like, quilts and pillows. It's flat the whole way across the lake."

"You're not thinking straight, kid."

"Nate! My name is Nate."

"Yeah, yeah, yeah, whatever. With that old Doo we'll be dawdling along. It's too far to Southend, in case you di'n't know."

"Yeah, I know, but —"

"And when Mr. Hothead gets here and sees our tracks heading out, he'll be on our tail in no time." Cal slapped one hand against the other. It was funny, thought Nate, how "if" had become "when" with regard to Shaker coming. Well, not really funny.

"So the sooner we get moving, the better," said Nate.

"You're not listening."

"The Doo can top sixty miles an hour."

"Hah!" said Cal. "Maybe thirty years ago when it rolled off the assembly line. And not pullin' a goddamned sled through new powder. While that Polaris —"

"Listen!" said Nate. He said it sharply and held his hand to his ear, managing to knock Cal clear off course.

They listened. "I don't hear nothin'," said the old man.

"Exactly!" said Nate. "We'd be able to hear him coming way up the trail, just like I heard you earlier. So we leave now and we get a good head start."

"That Polaris we borrowed from your next-door neighbor," said Cal, undaunted. "On a clear day like this, no headwind, that thing can top ninety."

But Nate was on his feet now. He'd never taken off his snow pants when he returned from his errands. Now he found his coat and started to put it on. "Here's the deal," he said. "You sit here while I get the sled hooked up. I load you in —" Cal started to interrupt, but Nate cut him off. His adrenaline was rising to the occasion. He wanted out so bad he could taste it. "I'll come around here, load you on. Then we listen again. If we don't hear any snowmobile coming, we have at least ten or fifteen minutes lead time."

"You're a raving psycho," said Cal.

"No, the psycho is the one who *you* said might be coming back here. And since I don't want to see anyone dying in this camp and making a mess of it — whether it's me, him, or you — I want to get out. It's that simple."

"Simple, hah!"

"And you'll be riding shotgun," said Nate. "He chases us, you can blow him up for all I care!"

Cal actually seemed to like that idea, but it didn't matter to Nate one way or another what the old man thought. He wanted out. He was breathing hard. His voice was scratchy. He needed water. He needed to load up some supplies if he was going to do this. And he needed to close the place up, good and tight. You never left the place open, vulnerable. You never left the fire-box empty; you never left without cleaning the fridge or without bear-proofing. You just didn't. Not for any reason. His shoulders fell, exhausted by the thought of it all. Then he started for the door.

"Nate, stop."

"No, *you* stop," Nate shouted. "No one invited you here. You don't make the decisions. Got that? It's my place. Mine and my father's and my mother's. It's our place. You aren't welcome here."

His voice was rough as sandpaper, but he seemed to have broken through at last. He actually thought Cal heard him.

Nate took a deep breath. His mitts were on the table. He reached for them, and his trapper's hat with the fur-lined earflaps.

Pulled them on. His father would understand about leaving like this. His father understood priorities.

"You was looking at my leg earlier," said Cal, his voice low, beaten.

Nate turned up the flap of his hat. "What'd you say?"

"My leg," said Cal, raising his voice. "You saw the burns."

"Yeah, I saw the burns. What's that got to do with anything?"

"It's got everything to do with everything," said Cal testily.

Nate threw back his head, ready to howl with frustration. "You burned down the frigging place. I've seen the burns on my dad's arms — the burns he got *dragging you to safety*. So what's your point?"

Cal glared at him. "When Shaker gets here and finds the place deserted, how you think he's gonna feel?" He waited. "You think he might be just a wee bit pissed off? Think he might wanna make somebody pay?" He raised his eyebrows. "How long did it take your daddy to build this place again?"

# Raising the Stakes

Nate took off his mitts and threw them on the table. He took off his hat and unzipped his quilted vest. Then he just hung his head, defeated.

"You know it's true," said Cal.

Nate managed a nod.

"Come here," said Cal quietly. "Sit down."

And because it was the kind of thing somebody who gave a damn might say, Nate responded. At the moment, he couldn't think of what else to do.

Cal reached over, grimacing as he did, and pulled the kitchen chair close, then patted the seat. Nate didn't trust the guy, but he didn't have the energy to pull the chair out of swatting distance. He didn't sit down so much as slump, like his skeleton had given up on him. He'd slept well enough, but he was bone weary and emotionally exhausted.

"I've made a dog's breakfast of my life, Nate. I lost my daughter, drove my son away, and eventually his mother." He stopped for a moment, as if maybe he hadn't thought of her for a long time. "She got out okay, went up to her folks. Your dad ever hear from her?" Nate shook his head. "I'm not surprised," said Cal. "She closed the door after her when she left." He tapped his forehead as if to suggest closing the door was some kind of metaphor for losing your marbles.

Cal looked at the gun lying across the chair in front of him. He fingered the stock, traced a line down to the trigger. "I never been all that good at makin' logical decisions about nothin'." He chuckled. "Just ask your father. On second thought, don't bother." He suddenly breathed in sharply through his teeth, making Nate look up to see him writhe in pain.

"Should I get you something?"

"I'm tempted to say the bottle, but I might need to be sober sometime today. Sharp. A little hand-eye coordination, you know what I mean? So, no. It's okay. I'm good."

Nate got up anyway, poured a glass of water, and got the Tylenol Extra Strength from the table. Handed them to Cal.

"Thanks," said the old man, but he just put the glass and the pills down on the arm. "What I said way back when about this gig here, this mess I got myself into — it was true. They offered me good money to help 'em out. I just wanted one last shot at gettin' the hell outa here. Oh, at first I figured this was the way to the big money, a chance to play with the big boys. It took gettin' shot to figure out they was just gonna use me up and spit me out. I ain't the sharpest knife in the drawer.

"But, see, I've got this buddy — the one man I can truly call a friend. He lives up in Yellowknife, up there in the territories. He said I could come anytime, share his place. And I figured if I could get myself up there, then I could close the door, like Dolores did. Your grandmother. Collect my old-age pension. Try to —"

"Hold it, hold it!" said Nate, throwing up his hands, his face strained as if he were Superman trying to stop a freight train. "I want to hear this story, Cal. Honest. But if you think Shaker is coming, maybe this isn't the time, right?" It took a moment, but Cal nodded. "So what do you say? Is he coming or were you just blowing smoke? Trying to scare me so I'd do what you want?"

Cal actually smiled. "Looks like you got me pegged."

"Just tell me," said Nate.

"Then, yeah, I think he's comin', all right, and I'll tell you why. When we was holed up in the loggin' camp waiting to be 'rescued,' he wouldn't stop talking about what he was going to do to you when he got the chance." Cal looked directly at Nate, and Nate searched his eyes for some telltale hint that this was just more guff. But it wasn't.

"He was talking trash, the kind of trash a guy talks when he's in lockup: What he's gonna do to the sons of bitches that put him behind bars. How he's gonna make it last, the torture. How it's not just gonna be painful but humiliatin'. *That* kind of crap." He shook his head. "He's one sick puppy. The kind of guy who'd rather get back at you than get away."

Again, Nate searched his grandfather's weathered face and saw only the truth.

"Come to think of it," said Cal. "That man *is* in jail." He tapped his head again.

"Okay," said Nate. "I get it. And if that's the case, I *really* don't want to hang around."

"But you don't want to lose this place either, right? You don't want some lunatic availin' himself of all that fuel you've got out in the shed and havin' hisself a marshmallow roast, do you?" Nate shook his head vehemently. "Which is why I'm gonna stay," said Cal, tapping himself on the chest.

Nate didn't speak. He hated admitting that this is what he wanted. Hated admitting that he didn't really care what happened to Cal, as long as he kept his word and was somehow able to stop Shaker from torching the place.

"Here's what I'll do," said Cal. "Forget about settin' up the armchair in here. I hear him comin', I set myself up out on the sunporch there, right by the outside door. The blind is down over it. He won't see me. You can stay or go; either way I'm going to take him down — but outside, where he won't make a mess." Nate made a face. "Dammit, boy, you can't have it both ways! This man is on your tail. He needs you as a hostage. If he stops here, I'll have the drop on him and soon as he's close enough I'll waste him. If he sees your tracks headin' out to the lake and takes after you, I'll just step out onto that stoop and — *boom!* — shoot him in the back. Not very sportsmanlike, I admit, but it gets the job done."

"Whoa! Stop!" said Nate, jumping to his feet. "This is like some dumb video game."

"I thought kids your age ate that stuff up."

"Yeah, sure: *Call of Duty, World of Warcraft.* But those are games. Fantasy. And what you're talking is . . . is real life. I know the difference."

Cal squinted. He was getting angry again. It didn't take much. "Yeah, well, what you call 'real life', it's different for some, eh? Not everybody gets to grow up with two workin' parents livin' in a nice big house up there near the university."

"Ah, jeez!" said Nate, smacking the top of the table with the flat of his hand. "Don't tell me you've been stalking us."

"Not stalking. I just drove by the place to take a gander. My *point* is that a bad man has his sights set on you and, one way or another, he's gonna want to make you pay. And what I'm sayin' is that I'm not gonna let him. You hear me?"

Cal had raised his voice so much, Nate figured even Shaker could hear him if he was within a ten-kilometer range. Nate nodded.

"So sit your ass down and let's finish this! And then you can take off or whatever you want. If we hear him comin', we'll play it by ear. But one"—he held up a crooked index finger—"he is not gonna get you. And two, he is not gonna get this camp."

His voice was firm. "And believe me, I can see the—whatever they call it—the *irony,* is that it?" Nate nodded. "I can see the irony of me saying what I just said. Got it. But still . . ."

And Nate realized something that hadn't even crossed his mind until that very moment. Cal had come back here to save him. This guy could have sped off into the forest any which way he wanted. He'd chosen to come back. Yeah, he was injured and needed somewhere to hole up. But that wasn't the whole picture. Meekly, Nate resumed his seat.

"I'll make this quick," Cal said. He was pale. Losing the battle, thought Nate. There was a bullet in the man's leg and it was doing him in. He glanced at the bandage and saw the growing stain. "There's something you oughta know," he said. He was about to go on, but he stopped and held up his hand as if to catch something. But it was his ear that was doing the catching. For an old man, his hearing was good. Nate had heard it, too: a snowmobile.

# WWDD?

Nate grabbed his mitts and hat and zipped himself up. He dropped first one mitt, then the other, then the hat as he raced toward the door. He almost fell trying to swoop them up, reached out to gain his balance, and banged his hand hard on the door handle. Swore like a trooper. Then flung open the door and stepped out onto the covered porch, pulling his hat down tight by the flaps.

"Nate!"

"What?"

"The shells?"

Cal had gotten up and was limping toward the door. Nate stared at him without a clue what he was talking about. "The shells!" he said again, louder, leaning hard against the door frame.

Cal held up the Remington. "I'm gonna need some ammo."

Nate pulled off his right mitt and dug the box of shotgun shells from his pocket. He was going to throw the box, but checked himself at the last second and handed it to Cal, who had to let go of the door frame to take it.

Cal smiled. "Five-fifty-six buckshot. This'll do 'er."

"Whatever," Nate said, and was out the sunporch door and into the blinding light.

He leaped on the Ski-Doo and stuck his feet in the stirrups. The key was already in the ignition, where he'd left it after his errands. He turned the key, squeezed the throttle, heard the engine rev, and then looked out toward the lake, squinting into the sun.

His goggles! His helmet!

He hadn't bothered with them when he was making his trip to the shed, but he was going to be driving into that sun the whole way. Instinctively, he let go of the throttle and was about to climb off the Doo, but as soon as the engine roar subsided to idle chatter, he heard the other machine, the one coming his way and getting nearer. There was no time to lose. He took one quick look behind to the trailhead, followed by a quick glance at the camp door. It was open a crack and he could see Cal there, see the tip of the gun barrel shining blue-black. Waiting.

There was a stairway just to the right of the sunporch leading down to the beach. It was invisible under a thick carpet of snow, and the quickest route out of the yard, though not one he'd have normally used. But down he went and out across the beach, which at some point became the lake, though it was impossible to tell where the one ended and the other began. He swerved past the water hole and gunned it.

When he was a hundred yards out, he slowed just enough to take a good look back, fully expecting to see the snowmobile in the yard by now. But the yard was empty.

He was still clinging to the chance that it wasn't Shaker after all, that it was the authorities or his father. He still had this hope he'd be able to turn back. He hated running away, hated leaving the camp like that — in the hands of a crazy, injured old coot. But what he hated most was that this old coot had laid a trap to kill someone and he, Nate, was *relying* on him to do it.

How had it come to this?

All around him was a day of bright sunshine, the air crisp, the sky achingly blue, and yet he felt as if he were right back in the middle of the nightmare, where somebody was going to die and the only vaguely good thing left to cling to was that, with any luck, it wasn't going to be him.

He looked back again. Nothing.

This was good, right? Surprising, but good. He imagined the hit man crashing into a tree and allowed himself the satisfaction of that fantasy for a moment or two before turning again. The yard was still empty. There was no way that noise on the track had been so far away that the sled wouldn't have arrived by now. He slowed down and brought the Ski-Doo around in a half turn so he didn't have to strain his neck. There was nothing in the yard. Then the sunroom door flew open and out hobbled Cal. He was holding up his arm with the gun in it, shaking it like a madman. He seemed to be trying to say something. For a moment Nate thought he was calling him back. Then Cal leaned over the rail of the stoop and pointed to his right, toward the Hoebeeks' camp.

And there he was.

The big black Polaris hit the hill down to the beach so fast Shaker got major air, then landed with a huge spray of new powder — and a rooster tail of it — as he sped out onto the lake.

It took a precious moment for Nate to process what was

happening. The guy had somehow guessed at the danger waiting for him and circled around it. Which meant Nate was on his own.

He pressed his thumb hard on the gas and swung the Ski-Doo toward the east passage. He ducked his head as low as he could to keep the wind out of his face, but his eyes were already streaming with tears and his vision was far from good. Shoulder-checking, he saw the Polaris gaining on him, cutting the angle. For a moment he imagined Dodge at the controls. It was one of their games, and because he was Dodge, he was playing to win. Oh, he'd have a grin on his face as big as Indiana. But it wasn't Dodge. And it wasn't a game.

*Bang!*

The sound of the gun rang out, loud. Nate ducked, then checked over his shoulder again.

*Bang!*

It was Cal shooting at Shaker! Unfortunately, by now buck-shot wasn't going to cut it; it'd have taken a marksman with a rifle and scope to stand a chance of hitting him.

*Bang!*

Picnic Island was straight ahead, not a hundred yards away. Nate veered to the left to pass it. He'd need a plan because there was no way he could outrace the Polaris.

*Crack!*

The sound of the handgun was different. A quick glance was all Nate needed to see that Shaker had his revolver out.

So much for needing a hostage!

Nate bent low, began to zigzag evasively, but not so much as to slow his forward progress or so wildly as to buck him off.

*Crack!*

He ducked even lower. *Is he aiming at the snowmobile? Does he need me or does he just want me dead?*

The powerful snowmobile had cut the distance between them by half, but now he seemed to be pulling out wide to Nate's left, planning on passing him — rounding him up — driving him in toward Picnic Island, maybe to crash on the rocks. He was almost even with him now; Nate only had to turn his head a little to the left to see the Polaris, not twenty yards east.

To his right, the sheer granite wall of the jumping cliff came into view, rising up five stories from the fresh new snow on the lake.

"Go for it, Numbnuts."

He could hear Dodge in his ear, as if he were riding tandem on the Doo. "Don't be such a wuss."

What was he going on about? Go for what?

*Crack!*

*Ping!*

The bullet hit the hood of the Doo, and in the shock of it Nate momentarily lost control. It was as if the old sled wanted him off! Wanted to shake this pesky critter riding him, like a bronco.

"It's your big chance, Nate the Great. You can do it."

This was not the time or place for a What Would Dodge Do? moment.

But wait! Maybe . . .

Even as he thought it, he realized it wasn't so much his "big" chance; it might be his only chance.

He veered away from the other snowmobile, veered toward the island, toward its southern point. He would get in as close as he could to shore, something you never did in a boat because of boulders that could tear off the prop. There! The last straggly chain of stones, like the tail of some dinosaur. The southern tip. And now around it, cutting it close, leaning in hard to the right, putting the island between him and the madman on his backside.

Shaker was caught off guard and took a minute to adjust. Good! He'd probably guess Nate was heading home. Was that an option? If he could get himself back to camp, maybe Cal could deal with the lunatic. But there was no way. No time.

In a matter of moments, he could see the wide expanse of open shoreline that marked the picnic place. A quick glance over his shoulder showed Shaker gaining on him again but also having lost some distance by swinging out too far and not anticipating Nate changing directions.

Then Nate was charging up the beach, past the fish-gutting stand, past the snow-covered table and the mound that was the built-up fire pit, slowing down to enter the bush, not as thick here as on the mainland, but not something you could power through at speed.

He knew where the trail started, the one he and Dodge had labored over during their last summer together, the trail that zig-zagged up the lazy slope following whatever natural trails there were, heading toward the jumping cliff. The Polaris was gaining on him. Nate knew where he was going, but Shaker didn't have a clue.

*Crack!*

Nate swerved inadvertently and his skis sideswiped a tree, which dumped a night's worth of snow on him. As he regained control, he almost hit another tree bending in over the trail, weighed down by the fall, and suddenly realized that trees could be down up ahead — something the Doo could not get over. He would be trapped!

But Dodge, sitting behind him, whispered in his ear. "You're in it now, Numbster. Make me proud!"

The trail climbed, a switchback, so that at one moment Nate

was no more than a car's width from Shaker with only sparse brush between them, Shaker speeding north while Nate sped south, passing each other on the slow ascent. Luckily, Shaker had pocketed his gun, needing both hands on the controls now, readying himself for the hairpin turn just ahead. He may have stashed his weapon, but the smile on his face was terrifying.

And then with one more turn to the right, heading almost due north, Nate reached the straightaway and sped up. He could barely see where he was going with the sun in his eyes, but he'd worked this stretch with Dodge — the runway for the big jump. And because he'd cared for his insane friend and hadn't wanted him to die, Nate had worked hard to make that runway smooth and straight so that Dodge would have maximum acceleration when he hit the lip of the precipice. Blind as Nate was, his eyes streaming with tears, he accelerated, pouring it on, squeezing every last bit of horsepower the Ski-Doo had in it, needing to pull ahead of Shaker and make him come on all the harder.

And there ahead was the dogleg right. He had to slow down to take it, even as his pursuer was speeding up. And then the sky opened up before him, the bush cleared to either side of him, the verge — the threshold — straight ahead. It was his only chance; he screamed toward it and then threw his body hard to the right, turning the handles with every last bit of strength he could muster, slewing the skis hard, hard, hard, feeling the tread grab at the soft new snow, not catching anything, not getting a grip, sliding sideways toward the cliff head. Nate was screaming, "No! No! No!" and behind him the ghost of Dodge was laughing hysterically. Then he felt it — the earth under the tread — and he gunned the motor, crashing the Doo into the brush and coming to a dead stop.

And he turned
in time to see
the Polaris sail out
over the edge
out over the lake.

Over the rumble of his idling engine, Nate heard Shaker
scream. Then he was floating in not-so-free fall, holding on to the
handles as if they could save him as the Polaris pulled him downward as sure as any anchor.

# The Weight

"Check it out," says Dodge. He's looking over the specs of the Hoebeeks' brand-new snowmobile. "Four hundred and seventeen pounds."

"What's that in real weight?" says Nate.

Dodge grins his dangerous grin, as if he is already thinking up new adventures. "A whole lot of muscle!" he says.

# The Opposite of Nothing

Nate sat on his Ski-Doo on the frozen lake, staring at the scene of the crime. Like a cat, the Polaris had landed on all fours, but it was not purring or making any sound at all. Probably used up quite a few of its nine lives.

Shaker lay on his back, an awkward snow angel, one leg draped over the seat of the snowmobile and his left arm bent in a way that suggested that, angel or not, flying was going to be out of the question. His upper torso was deep in the snow, which may have saved his life; Nate couldn't tell yet because he was too afraid to go near him, as still as he was, lying there twenty yards away. He might be dead. He might be in shock. He might be faking it until Nate was near enough to grab. Nate pulled up beside the Polaris, reached over, took the key, and pocketed it. Then he drove the Doo out in a big circle and came as close as he could get to the victim on the other side of the sled. Through the broken visor of

Shaker's helmet, he saw the shattered remains of the silver Gucci shades and, beneath them, a face caked in blood. Looking at the cracked windshield of the Polaris, Nate could see what had happened: the sled making contact and Shaker — still hanging on — crashing, crumpling. He felt woozy all of a sudden, like he was on a sinking ship. Afraid the madman might wake up at any moment and take Nate down with him, the way a drowning man can take down his rescuer. He edged his snowmobile closer, until he could reach out and move Shaker's good arm and lay it across his chest. It was limp, dead weight. Then he edged closer still and hit the kill switch on the Ski-Doo. He took off his left mitt. Hanging on with his right hand, he leaned out over the body and pressed his index and middle fingers on Shaker's carotid artery. It was directly under the talons of the tattooed eagle diving for a kill. There was a pulse there. Nate snatched his fingers away as if he had touched something scorching hot. It was not hot, just his fear was. After a moment, he was ready to try again, although without a watch, it would be hard to guess at the man's heart rate. Then he noticed that on the arm lying across the man's chest was a big honking Rolex. He shimmied it off Shaker's wrist. Then he pressed his two fingers against the artery again and counted the beats over fifteen seconds: twelve, which multiplied by four meant a heart rate of forty-eight. The cold was already getting to him. Not good. Not much blood was reaching his brain. Meanwhile, Nate's own hand was freezing from exposure. He quickly put on his mitt again. There was nothing he could do here. Nothing. He started up the Ski-Doo and headed back to the camp.

"You wanna do what?"

Nate was gathering his goggles and helmet. "I'm going back for him."

"That friggin' killer?"

Nate didn't bother responding. He was in a hurry. It was close to twenty below outside. Every moment wasted meant more frostbite damage.

Cal was sitting in the chair by the fire doing some serious damage to the bottle of scotch. "Think of this, Florence Nightingale," he said. "You'll be doin' the world a favor if you take a good long time gettin' there."

Nate strode toward the door. He'd had about as much of Cal's philosophy as he could take, but there wasn't time to wrangle with him. Outside, he drove the Doo over to the shed, where he hooked up the trapper sled. It was just over six feet long, two feet across, and two feet deep. It should do the job, except that in freezing weather the spring-loaded hitch wasn't as easy to attach as his dad made it look. The process ate up precious minutes. Part of what made him mad about what Cal said was that he, Nate, was fighting the same impulse. Why should he rescue this guy? He couldn't quite explain it. But when he'd taken the advanced first-aid course, he'd been excited about maybe actually doing something in an emergency rather than just being the quickest person to punch in 911. He didn't have that option here. It was this or nothing. And nothing didn't sit well with him.

Finally, he was ready. By Shaker's fat Rolex it had been nearly thirty minutes since he left him. He shook his head; there was nothing else he could do but try. Maneuvering the body onto the sled was going to be hard. He only wished he still had his snowshoes. And who had stolen those? Talk about irony.

Shaker's face looked waxy. Nate reached out to touch the skin; it felt as stiff as old putty. He felt again for a heartbeat. Nothing. He waited a whole minute. Was there anything at all? Was he imagining something too faint to really count and at too great an interval to do much good at all?

With a lot of effort, he piled the body onto the sled. The man was built like a middle linebacker and probably weighed as much — which made him about fifty pounds heavier than Nate. He had brought cam straps, a snake's nest of them from the container they kept in the back of the Mule. The straps were to serve a double purpose: one, to hold the man down so he didn't bounce out of the sled or slide out when the sled headed up the hill to the camp; and two, to hold him down in case he came back to life. As he was tying the last strap in place, Nate remembered the nasty black revolver. He checked Shaker's pockets; it didn't seem to be on him. He checked again for a cell phone. Nothing. He looked out at the wide expanse of snow around him, still sparkling like all get out. Made him think of a Johnny Cash song his dad liked, "Field of Diamonds." The weapon was probably out there somewhere, buried, where it would stay until spring. And when the ice finally melted, with any luck it would sink to the bottom of the lake.

By the time he'd gotten the body back to the camp, Shaker was dead. Nate stood beside the sled pulled up close to the stoop. He checked Shaker's pulse a couple of times and felt nothing at all. He hadn't saved him.

He stared down at the man for a few minutes. Then he looked at the watch he'd taken from him: it was 2:23. There was no way they'd catch the Budd now. Which was when it snapped. Everything he'd been holding in, the huge adrenaline rush of the ride up to the jumping cliff and everything that had happened since. He had killed a man. He could have died himself. And the floodgates opened. At some point, he felt a hand on his shoulder, leading him inside and closing the door behind them.

# Delirium

Nate woke up disoriented. Not spatially; he knew this little box of a room as well as he knew his own bedroom back home. He was disoriented in time. For a moment, he didn't know *when* he was.

It was the light. The light sifting in the curtained window was wrong somehow. It wasn't summer light. It wasn't morning light. It was coming from the wrong direction. A watch. He was wearing a watch. Then he remembered — felt — the clunky Rolex he'd taken off Shaker's thick, limp wrist, and lifting his arm to the light, he saw that it was five o'clock. Late afternoon.

But what day?

Cal was asleep by the stove. The scotch bottle was empty. The cabin was cooling down. Nate heaped some wood on the embers in the stove. He looked at Cal's sleeping face. Some faces in repose were neutral. Some, like his mother's, looked peaceful. Even when no one was looking, Astrid Ekholm smiled. But there was no peace in Cal's face. His features were strained. He looked like a man in a tug-of-war that never ended. He was sweating, too, despite the chill in the air. The wound had seeped right through the old sweats Nate had found for him. The bandage would need changing. But sleep was good, even if it took a bottle of booze to get there. And it wasn't exactly as if he craved the man's company.

He wandered over to the little window in the east wall that looked out onto the yard. There stood the sled with the dead body strapped to it. Crap. He'd have to do something about that. He turned away and stopped. Closed his eyes and took a long, deep breath, in and out. Night was coming. He'd have to do something about it right now.

Dressed warmly, he set off. He fired up the Doo. He cleared a place on the workshop floor, found an old paint-stained drop cloth. Then he dragged the corpse into the shed and laid him out, covered him over. He stood and stared at the bundle in the dimming light. He didn't think the drop cloth would keep the mice from him for long.

He shuddered.

He had killed this man. He had deliberately led him up a treacherous path to a sheer and hazardous drop. He had taken his own life into his hands, true, but he had lived and Shaker had not. It was not something he could have ever imagined doing in a million years. He closed his eyes again and lowered his head in prayer. But his prayer didn't get all the way to God. It was a prayer to his friend Dodge. "You saved my life, man," he said. Then he opened his eyes and shook his head slowly in bewilderment. The idea of Dodge saving anybody's life seemed so totally whacked out he almost laughed. He didn't want to do that. Hysteria didn't seem far off.

He was about to leave the shed when he suddenly turned,

found the padlock, closed the door, and locked the dead man inside. He wasn't taking any chances.

With renewed energy, Nate collected the plywood shutters in the sled and drove them over to the H-house. He had brought along some supplies from the work shed, so before he put the shutters back up, he screwed in several pieces of one-by-six across the back door to keep it tightly closed. By the time he'd replaced the shutters, the sun was just a yellow crayon line along the western hills and the deep cold was settling in. He was hungry, but he felt a little bit better. At least one camp was shipshape.

"A little better" didn't last long. When he stepped into the house, Cal was groaning and thrashing his head from side to side. Nate took off his outdoor clothes and made his way over to the old man. The tug-of-war wasn't going well. His expression was of a man in mortal pain. Sweat poured from his ragged face. Nate knelt and hesitantly leaned toward the sopping red bandage. The smell made him gag: a putrid smell, the smell of tissue breaking down, infection setting in.

Nate stood up, stepped back two, three paces. When was this going to stop? Was he going to have two dead men on his hands by the end of the day?

"Kid," said Cal. He'd opened one eye, which was trained on Nate. He reached out for his arm, except that his hand fell short, landing with a thump on the arm of the chair. "I need help," he said.

"I'll change the bandage," said Nate.

Cal's mouth hung open. He shut it, and Nate watched the old man's stringy throat constrict as he tried to summon up some spit. "You gotta take me somewhere."

"There is nowhere. The Budd's been and gone."

Cal's eye closed. It seemed to take him some minutes to

register the news. Or to accept it. Then he opened both his eyes. "You gotta get me help."

Nate nodded, and then he said, without a trace of irony or anger, as if he were just asking a reasonable question, "How am I going to do that?"

Cal's eyes closed again. He became still and Nate wondered if he was finally facing his fate, the enormity of the mess he'd gotten himself into. Then he opened his eyes again.

"Likely," he said.

"What?"

"Likely La Cloche."

"What about him?"

"Down at Sanctuary Cove."

"Yeah, I know, but —"

"He's got a radiophone."

The information caught Nate off guard. He actually knew Likely had a phone. There'd been a couple of times when his mother or father had used it. He just hadn't thought about it.

"Nate, are you listening?"

"Yeah, yeah. But is he there?"

Cal swallowed hard and the muscles in his face strained. "It don't matter."

"I mean, how could he be with this snow and him being disabled and —"

"I said it don't matter! It don't matter whether he's there or not. I know where he keeps his keys."

Nate wasn't sure why he was surprised. And here he'd thought they were somehow special up at the north end. Cal probably knew where everybody kept their keys.

"Don't zone out on me, kid."

"Sorry. I . . . Yeah, so . . ."

Cal reached out his hand to Nate and managed to snag his arm, but he was too weak to hold on to it and his hand fell to his lap. His eyes appealed to Nate. "Please," he said. Nate didn't actually hear the word but saw the shape of it on the old man's lips. Probably not a word he'd used all that often.

"Okay," said Nate. "I'll go, except I don't know how to use a radiophone."

Somehow, even in dire pain, Cal managed a scowl. And seeing it was almost a relief. There was life in the old bastard yet.

Nate wasn't going anywhere without changing Cal's dressing. An argument ensued, but Nate was holding all the cards. The sweatpants he had lent Cal were toast. He rolled them down. Cal was harder to move now than before because he seemed to have no strength at all to help out. The upside was that he had no fight left in him to struggle.

Nate breathed through his mouth, avoiding the worst of the stink as he cut away the bandages. Wearing a pair of rubber washing-up gloves he found under the sink, he balled up the soggy dressing and hurled it in the woodstove, where it sputtered and bubbled. Gross.

He was about to hurl the sweatpants in, too, but didn't want to smother the fire. He put them in a garbage bag he'd deal with later. The wound looked every bit as bad as it had before, even more livid in color. He cleaned up the surface with wipes and then applied the ointment and new compresses and the rest of the bandage roll. Then he found another pair of old torn, paint-stained sweats, put them on Cal, and stopped to take a breather.

He looked at the eggs and bacon sitting on the table. They'd been out all day, abandoned. He was starving, but he didn't have the time to cook. So he made himself a sandwich: peanut butter and some old blueberry jam that had crystallized. It was from a batch Fern Hoebeek had made the previous year. He'd harvested the blueberries along with Dodge and Trick down by the dam, and Dodge had pretended a bear was coming just to get Trick's goat.

The bread was dry with blue mold spots. Too bad. There wasn't time to toast it, so he wolfed the sandwich down anyway and ended up gagging. Lukewarm water was all he had to wash it down with. The invaders had left a couple beers in the fridge but that, he figured, was the last thing he needed. If he made it through tonight, he might just want one later. Then he went to look at a large-scale map of the lake on the wall. There was Sanctuary Cove on the eastern shore, almost at the southernmost end of the lake.

"For Christ's sake, kid, what are you doin'?"

Cal's sleep had obviously reawakened his foul nature.

"Coming," said Nate, but he kept staring at the map. He wondered whether this is what a wild-goose chase looked like.

"If killin' me is what you had in mind, you're doin' a good job."

"You're the one who got himself shot," said Nate.

Which set Cal off, more foulmouthed than ever — a regular Vesuvius of red-hot resentment. His eyes closed and his body taut with pain, he still managed to hurl abuse at everything and everyone who'd ever crossed him or let him down. Untouched by any of it, Nate watched with rude fascination. And he thought of his father. He believed Burl Crow to be about as good a man as ever walked the earth. Listening to Burl's father bluster and rage, Nate's esteem for his own father only grew. How did any human manage to overcome such a start in life? Amazing.

The rant ended. The room grew quiet but for the ticking of the fire Nate had stoked up. He'd be gone a good long time.

"You still here?" said Cal.

"No," said Nate. "I'm gone."

# Sanctuary Cove

Oh, the stars.

There was the Ram truck constellation and . . . what were the other heavenly patterns they'd named? Gandalf, Donkey Kong, Larry Bird —

"Who?"

"The greatest basketball player *ever*," says Dodge. He points out a bunch of stars that are supposed to be Bird's elbow and knee and fingertips. "He's making a fadeaway jump shot — see the ball arcing toward the net?" The net was a star just off to the left, several million light-years away.

"Oh, right," says Nate. "I see him now. But he looks more like LeBron, to me."

"You're crazy, Numbster. Gotta be Larry. See? He's white."

The moon rose over the low-slung hills to the southwest, not full but with fullness in mind, fat with light, making the snow cover glitter and lending the abandoned Polaris a sharp and reaching shadow as Nate flew past it and on down the narrows.

Then he was riding across Dead Horse Bay, and Nate steered close to the shore but not too close, fearful of what he might see, for this was where the Hoebeeks had met their fate, where Dodge might still be floating, suspended in the dark. And maybe his ghost roamed the rocky shoreline, back and forth, back and forth, a spirit packed and waiting for his ship to come in and yet never ready to go. Nate tore his eyes from the dark shore, gripped the controls tighter.

And on and on he flew under the moon and stars.

"Do it," Dodge whispered in his ear. "What could go wrong?"

And Nate felt the excitement in the lost voice and obeyed his ghostly friend, flipping off the Ski-Doo's headlight. It was like diving down into the lake, flippers kicking, calf muscles straining, down into the darkness of night fish. It freaked him out but Dodge held him to the darkness. "Not yet," he said as Nate reached for the toggle. "A little longer."

Everything was a game of chicken to Dodge.


The shadowy settlement at Sanctuary Cove came into view off to his left, hugging the shore and marching up into the trees. No lights. Nobody home. Nate turned the sled shoreward. He knew about where Likely's place was, but he'd never come at it in the dark. He slowed as he got nearer to shore and turned southward, trying to pick out the place in a ghost town.

And then there it was, larger than the Crows' camp, impressive in silhouette. Nate found his way up the rise from the lake toward the small porch, but there would be no entrance from there; the snow was up to the door's window. So he made his way along the right flank of the cabin, in the lee of the storm, now passed, and around to the back, where there was a second entrance. Which wasn't going to be much easier to access. There was a shed back there as well, its door facing south and mostly clear of snow. He hoped like crazy there was a shovel in it, or it was going to be a very long night. There was a generator in there, something he wouldn't have known if Cal hadn't called out to him just as he was leaving.

"You got a flashlight?" Nate had stopped in the open door, sighed, and dropped his head. Somehow Cal managed to summon up a derisive little laugh. "Mr. Outdoorsman obviously di'n't teach you much about being prepared."

Nate had reached up then with both hands to the lintel of the door to support himself. Not because he was going to fall over but because he needed to keep his hands engaged at something other than wringing Cal's neck. He recalled how, back at the H-house, the man had grabbed his neck from behind in a pincer-like grip. How easy it would be to do the same thing to him. Finish the job off.

When Cal had wrung about as much out of the moment as he could, he explained about the generator, how the phone wouldn't work without electricity and how he'd have to switch the charge over from AC to DC in the La Cloche camp and where to find the switch to do that.

Assuming he could get the generator started.

Assuming the Doo didn't die on him on the way there.

"Is that everything?"

Cal had nodded, closed his eyes again. "Knock yourself out."

The keys were where Cal said they'd be and he got the generator going, and there was a shovel and Nate took to digging his way to the back door like a man possessed. The idea that on the other side of it was the possibility of contact with the world beyond this nightmare put new muscle into his back. He'd pay for this tomorrow, he thought — probably be sore for a week — but that didn't matter now. All that mattered was getting inside and finding the phone. Pray to God the phone worked. That the storm hadn't torn down the radio tower. That would just about be Nate's luck.

He stood inside the deeper dark of Likely's kitchen not having any idea which way to turn. He reached out, found a counter right where he'd expect to. So far, so good. Then his hand sidled up the wall until it made contact with a plastic switch plate.

And, lo, there was light.

He entered the front room, turning on lights as he went, and off to the side, where Cal said it would be, was a nook and there was the phone. Cal had told him what to do. How to get access to the tower, what buttons to push, but he didn't make the call right away. There was a time limit, and he needed to clear his head. Just the essentials, he told himself. Say only what you need to say.

His mother answered.

"Mom, it's me. I'm okay. I'm calling from a radiophone at Likely La Cloche's camp. There's only three minutes. You have to say 'over' when you finish talking. Over."

"Nate! Oh my God. What's happened?"

She didn't say "over," but he figured she was too surprised. He pressed the talk button. "Everything's okay. Did you get a text message from me? Over."

"No. I don't think so. When? Over."

"It'd have been a couple days ago. Never mind. A whole lot of things have happened and there isn't time to go into it now. Over."

It was his father on the extension when he took his thumb off the talk button. "Good to hear your voice, son. If you're at Likely's, you're in good hands. You say everything's okay and I'm hoping that means the camp is still standing. Over."

Nate smiled to himself. He forgot sometimes that he wasn't really an only child. He had this older sister, the camp.

"Likely's not here, Dad. I had to break in. The camp's still standing. But one of the escapees from the Sudbury Jail is dead. The one named Shaker. I've got him laid out in the work shed back at the camp. I'm not sure what to do about that. And I know the Budd doesn't run tomorrow so I'm not sure what to do next. Over."

There was a pause and then Nate realized that even though he'd said "over," he hadn't let go of the talk button.

"Let me make sure I heard you right," said his father, while on the other extension his mother said, "You've got a dead man lying in the work shed?"

"Yeah. And Calvin Crow is up here. I mean back at the camp. He's been shot. He'll need medical attention. What do I do now? Over."

His mother was saying "Oh, God. Oh, God. Oh, God," with Nate's name thrown in now and then. "We'll contact the authorities," said his father. "Can you stay there until I get back to you? Over."

"Stay where? Over."

"At Likely's — just until I phone you back."

"Yeah. I guess. But hurry, okay? It's freezing here. And I need to get back to him . . . to Cal . . . Over."

There was a pause at the other end — just electrically charged air buzzing and crackling in the line. Had he been disconnected? Nate pushed the talk button again. "Here's La Cloche's number," he said, and read it out. "Over."

"Good man," said Dad. "Sit tight."

"Love you, kid," said Mom. "Hang in there, you hear?"

"Over and out," said Dad.

He lit a fire. He had no idea how long they'd be getting back to him, but even if it was only minutes, he was shaking like a leaf in a nor'wester. He sat cross-legged on the floor in front of the flames, rocking back and forth like a crazy person. The relief of speaking to his parents — of handing off some of the responsibility — had felt really good for a few moments, but in some weird way, it had undone him. Again. And he wasn't sure how many undoings a person could go through before there was nothing left of him to unravel. He'd been holding on so tight, afraid to let go, afraid to give up. Now he just wanted to be home.

"Enough already!" he shouted into the empty camp. Then, not able to sit still any longer, he got up and walked around, touching things and picking things up and generally trying to keep from screaming.

There was a cane hanging on a kitchen chair at the table. Nate took it by its worn handle. He remembered seeing Mr. La Cloche with crutches. He got around pretty well on them. Didn't seem to slow him down. He raised the cane, squeezing it tight, and was glad Cal Crow was a long way away right then because the temptation to hit him would have been too much. Then the phone rang. His father, all business. Told him the medevac probably wouldn't get there until morning and the cops would come separately. They'd bring him out. "There's a manhunt for those guys," said his father. "Is it safe to go back to the camp? Is the other escapee still around? Over."

Nate hadn't really even thought of this. He only knew what Cal had said. He'd heard a shot and a scream but had assumed

Beck wasn't dead, although he was probably in custody. He'd have to go with that. "Yeah, it's safe," he said, deciding that "I think so" wasn't going to cut it. "I'll get back there right away."

"Are you sure? Why not camp out there? I'll get in touch with La Cloche, let him know what's up. Over."

Nate looked around. No. He'd had enough of other people's places. "I'm okay, Dad. I came down here on the Doo and she's running perfectly. Over."

"Good man," said his father. "Over."

"See you soon," said Nate. "Over and out." And he took his thumb off the talk button one last time.

He pushed the Ski-Doo hard on the way, took as straight a line as he could, wondering all the while if there would be a dead man sitting in front of a dead fire when he got there.

# A Turn for the Worse

Cal was standing at the stove, cooking bacon and eggs.

"Saw your light," he said without looking up as Nate entered the camp, bringing a good piece of night coldness in with him.

The aroma of the bacon and coffee made him weak in the knees. He struggled out of his outerwear, leaving it where it lay on the floor. But by the time he'd shaken the starlight out of his eyes, the scene had changed. Cal still stood before the propane stove with one hand on his hip and the other wielding a spatula, but he wasn't doing anything with the spatula; it hung motionless in the air over the frying pan, and when Nate looked closer he saw that the man, for all his jaunty stance, was shaking from head to toe. And then he fell.

Nate raced around the table, pushing the big chair out of his way. He flipped off the gas burners and then knelt down beside the old man. He was convulsing. Nate took him by the shoulders and half carried, half dragged him to the chair. Once he'd gotten him seated, he propped up his leg and was about to cover him when he felt Cal's forehead and realized he was already feverish. His breathing was fast and ragged. He felt Cal's chest; his heart was beating fast.

Nate stood over the man, breathing heavily himself. *Septic shock.* The words came to him from his Red Cross training, but nothing much came along with them. All he knew was that the bullet in his leg had to come out. And it had to come out now. He buried his head in his hands. How? How was he supposed to do this?

*Leave it to the medics.*

He looked at Cal's face, pain tugging at every muscle. His mouth open in a silent scream. He looked down the man's throat, and what came swimming into his mind was the image of a gut-hooked bass. One of those greedy buggers you didn't know you had on the line until it was too late and they'd swallowed the hook down into their gullet.

And that's when he knew what he had to do.

The fire in the woodstove had burned low, but the water in the kettle was still steaming. Nate raced to the corner behind the door where the fishing gear was stored. He found his tackle box and opened it up, grabbed his needle-nose pliers, and raced back to the kettle. He dropped the pliers into the kettle to disinfect them, then he turned back to Cal and tore off his sweatpants and the dressing, exposing the wound. He only looked at it long enough to figure out whether he'd have to open it up larger than the bullet hole. If he did, he'd need his filleting knife. Strange. Two days ago he'd been prepared to use one on this man — an intruder — and he couldn't do it. Now he was going to have to.

He threw the knife in the hot water as well and went to get the first-aid kit.

The water was too hot to put his hands into to recover his surgery equipment, which was a good thing, really. But he'd need to clean himself up. So he poured some of the steaming water into a big white enamel washbowl and added as little cold as possible. Then he lathered up as best he could, flinching at the heat, loving it, too, as it helped to melt away some of the stress. He grabbed the knife and the pliers, pulling them out with a pair of tongs, and laid them down on a clean tea towel. He found a stack of other clean towels to have on hand. This was going to get messy. He wished there was some kind of sedative he could give his patient, but Cal had drunk it all.

Nate knelt on the floor staring at the wound, knowing he was as likely to kill the man as save him. But to do nothing was to reduce the choices to one. So once again, he chose the opposite of nothing.

Standing over Cal with his bright-yellow washing-up gloves on, holding his pliers and his filleting knife, he said, "This is going to hurt." He wasn't quite sure who he was saying it to.

Nate entered the front room into bright sunlight. It didn't look much like an operating room. Didn't smell like one, either. Still smelled like bacon. He had eaten all of what Cal had cooked up, right after the surgery, without sitting down. Just stood there at the stove picking up the warm, greasy pieces out of the pan with freshly washed fingers and popping each strip into his mouth one after the other, his hands shaking. He'd eaten the cold eggs from the spatula, too tired to get himself a plate and utensils. Then he'd wiped his chin on his T-shirt and stumbled off to bed and instant oblivion.

His patient wasn't dead.

His chest was rising and falling. His temperature seemed to have dropped. But his face was ghostly pale. Nate had rebandaged the wound after pouring all that was left of the rubbing alcohol on the site. He hadn't had the energy to find Cal yet another pair of old pants, so he'd covered him with blankets. It was all he could do.

There was a lot of blood. On the floor, the chair, the blankets — on pretty much every towel they owned. His tools lay on the floor, marked with drying gore. The bullet lay in a small enamel bowl. He wondered if it would be used as exhibit A in a future murder trial. He hadn't put the bullet in Cal's leg, but he couldn't help thinking maybe he'd finished Shaker's job for him.

He looked again at Cal, his mouth closed, his face surly in repose but not, it seemed, in pain. And suddenly, unable to stop himself, Nate started to laugh. Couldn't help it. He shook with it, covered his mouth with both hands to stop it bursting out. Finally, he leaned on the table, shaking his head as the surge of it dissipated.

Spring break.


"You need to know somethin'." The voice in the room caught Nate off guard. "You need to know what happened."

Nate was tidying up, checking out the sunporch window every few minutes for the medevac copter, hardly bothering to look at his patient for fear he'd take a turn for the worse. Everything else had the last few days. But now here was the patient actually talking.

"You hear me, Nathaniel?"

Nate pulled a chair over from the table and sat by his side, quietly, slowly, as if the slightest noise or rapid movement might do the old man in.

"Yeah. I'm here."

"Listen good."

"Let me get you some water."

"No. Just sit. Listen."

So Nate listened, and all he heard for most of a minute was the man's breathing, but he could see something in his face, even though Cal's eyes were closed. He could see a coming together of something. Cal was preparing to tell him some terrible thing — he could feel it. And it disturbed him more than he could say, frightened him. It was hard to believe anything good could come out of Cal's mouth. And that turned out to be true.

# The Hard Truth

"Did your dad tell you what happened? What really happened?"

"What do you mean?"

"When them fool neighbors of yours come up here. The day they all died."

Nate shook his head, and not hearing him reply, Cal managed at last to open one of his eyes.

"Burl didn't tell you?"

"Well, yeah. I mean I think I know what happened. I'm just not sure what you're getting at."

Cal nodded. He swallowed and made a face. Nate got him a glass of water and Cal accepted it, drank a few drops as if it were the last thing in the world he really wanted.

"Likely La Cloche told me about what happened," he said. "'Bout the three of them arriving there. Him standing out on the dock trying to talk sense into . . . what was his name?"

"Hoebeek. Art Hoebeek."

"Right. Art. I remember that now. Likely told 'em it was a damn fool thing to do, the weather could change anytime, he'd put their fridge up for them until —"

"I know all that," said Nate.

Cal stopped. Took another sip of water from the glass, some of it dribbling down his chin.

"Okay," he said. "But I wonder if your dad saved you from your friend's part in it."

"Dodge?"

"Right. The boy you was pretending to be when I barged in on you over there." Weakly, he cast his hand in the direction of the Hoebeeks' camp.

Nate shook his head. "No," he said quietly. "He didn't tell me that."

"Figured as much," said Cal. He looked down for a moment, and then his eyes refocused on Nate and it felt to Nate as if he were being strapped into his chair.

"I won't waste your time," said Cal. "Ol' Likely pretty well had Hoebeek turned around. He was seeing sense. Nodding instead of shaking his head. Which is when Dodge calls his dad over, takes his arm, and walks him down the dock a bit, away from La Cloche." Cal's face clouded over and Nate held his breath at what was coming. As if in just a moment he were going to hear Dodge's voice, just as he'd been hearing it the last few days and in his nightmares for going on five months.

"What?" he said.

Cal maneuvered himself into a sitting position. "Likely's an old geezer, so folks maybe think he don't hear so good." Cal shook his head. "That kid . . ." He shook his head again. "He says, 'Dad, don't be such a wuss.' Something like that. Maybe it was 'don't be such a pussy.'"

Cal turned away and then quickly glanced sidelong at Nate, with a look in his eye as if expecting Nate to argue with him — deny what he'd said. Nate just stared back at him, waiting, already knowing somehow what was coming.

"So Art, he starts to say something to the boy and Dodge just cuts him off. Just wipes his hand through the air and the old man stops. 'He's a gimp, Dad.' That's what he said. 'Are you going to let some old cripple tell you what you can and can't do?'"

Nate sat motionless, cold all over. Started shaking his head.

"I'm only tellin' you what Likely La Cloche told me," said Cal. "Swear to God."

"No," said Nate, almost under his breath. Then he said it again, more firmly. "No." He stared daggers at Cal.

Cal was a liar and a crook — a mean-spirited scoundrel. But even in his weakened state, he held Nate's gaze, and Nate could see nothing in the old man's eyes of malice or spitefulness. Right here, right now, he was telling Nate the unvarnished truth. And Nate knew it. He could hear it. Hear those words coming out of Dodge's mouth.

"That's so . . . so . . ."

"Stupid? Damn straight, it's stupid," said Cal, thumping the arm of the chair with his hand. "But I'll tell you what was a whole lot stupider." He leaned forward. "His old man agreeing with him," he said. Then he leaned back again, exhausted and with a look in his eye Nate hadn't seen before that looked an awful lot like sorrow. As if this is how it all happens, all the time. You know all the reasons not to and then someone convinces you to do it anyway.

There was nothing to say. All Nate could think of, suddenly, was Trick, Dodge's little brother. A worrywart, frightened of his own shadow, but smart and funny and full of imagination. Enough imagination to know what could go wrong. What did he say, or did he get to say anything? Nate didn't dare ask. Couldn't bear to know. Knew anyway.

He slumped in his chair, looked down at his hands loosely clasped in his lap. He was too weak to hear more. Powerless. Behind it, a wave of hopeless anger was building, but then it subsided almost immediately. What was the point?

"I'm sorry."

He looked up and Cal was staring at him. "I figured maybe your dad wouldn'ta told you that." He waited and Nate nodded. And Cal nodded back at him. "I figured you needed to know, is all."

And the two of them sat there then, with nothing left to say until the medevac copter came and took Calvin Crow away.

# WWND?

The de Havilland Beaver seemed to tumble out of the sky, skimming down the hills behind the camp and landing on the lake off the north shore. The pontoons of summer had been replaced by skis. Once it had finished landing, it turned and made its way toward the camp. Nate stood on the seat of the Ski-Doo down on the beach, waving at the plane like a survivor at sea on a raft.

The plane was deep-blue and white with gold stripes and the word POLICE in caps along the fuselage. Seeing Nate, the plane angled toward him and approached until it was about as far out as the swim raft usually sat. Then the engines were turned off and the revs slowed down until you could make out the shape of the propeller. Nobody did anything for a minute or so. From the passenger-side door, an Ontario Provincial Police officer stepped out onto the strut and waved at Nate, although his eyes were surveying the yard, the sunporch, the trees, and Nate realized that, to the cops, he could just as easily be a decoy as a kid who was utterly alone. No wonder they'd stopped so far out.

Satisfied, the officer threw a pair of snowshoes down onto the snow, put them on. From the back of the plane, another figure emerged through the passenger-side door. It was Burl.

A second officer stepped out and handed down a rifle to the first. Both of the officers approached Nate with their rifles aimed at the ground but ready for anything.

Nate embraced his father and neither of them said a word. Then he looked at the first officer and said, "The dead guy's in the shed."

There was enough room for both Nate and the corpse in the de Havilland. They'd brought along a body bag. Nate craned his neck to look behind him at its flat blackness, imagining himself inside there. It could have gone that way. He had a lot of explaining to do. Meanwhile, the cops had been to visit Cal in the hospital. He had even more explaining to do. And there was a guard at the door to make sure he didn't get any ideas about leaving.

Nate looked out the window as the plane lifted off, leaving the glittering, snow-covered lake behind. They'd be back again on the weekend, his dad said. Up Saturday, back down Sunday. Astrid would come as well; they'd make an outing of it: spring cleaning.

"You cool with that?" his dad asked.

Nate nodded. There was that old adage about getting back on a horse as soon as possible once you'd been thrown.

"Maybe we should ask Paul to come," said Burl. Nate paled, but his father only raised his eyebrow a little. Then he narrowed his eyes at Nate, and there was as much fear in his expression as there was reproach. And there was relief in it, too. This could have all gone so terribly wrong.

There was no chance to talk further in the plane because of the engine noise, and Nate was left alone with his thoughts. All too clearly, he could see Dodge manipulating his foolish father. He could see him bullying Trick into submission. Taking over. And what would Nathaniel Crow have done at that moment? He would never know, and it would probably haunt him forever.

# The Passenger

Nate wasn't sure what woke him up that night at the camp. It wasn't any nightmare. He listened to the silence, heard the sound of his parents breathing on the other side of the wall. There was no threat in this darkness. No snowmobiles racing through the woods toward them. No ghosts.

He climbed out of his bed and entered the front room. He filled up the Ashley, left the door open a moment, enjoying the leaping flames. Then he closed it up and walked out onto the sunporch. The weather had broken over the last week. It was still below freezing at night, but the melt was on. Real spring was on its way, a month or so later than for anybody else in the world, it seemed.

He slipped on his gum boots and stepped outside. The sky was wheeling with stars, but he was looking for one particular constellation. Where was it? There. The Ram truck. He picked out the headlights, the gun rack, the taillights. And there was George Star at the wheel, bright as ever. But there was another star there, too, faint but holding its own. It looked as if George had picked himself up a passenger.

# AFTERWORD

My first novel for young adults, *The Maestro*, was written in 1995. Among various titles it garnered as it was published elsewhere were *The Survival Game*, in the United Kingdom, and *The Flight of Burl Crow*, in Australia. The story was about both those things: an act of survival and a flight — an escape — from cruelty. To this day, kids still write me to ask what happened to Burl, and they often add suggestions as to what should happen to his nasty father, Calvin Crow. For quite a while I thought of writing a sequel but . . . well, I never got around to it. Then suddenly, just a couple of years ago, I had a good idea for a sequel — part of an idea, anyway. And when I mentioned it to my wife, Amanda Lewis, she supplied the crucial *second* idea that made it impossible *not* to write this book. Except so much time had gone by that Burl would have been old enough to have a teenage son of his own. Great! I'd write an intergenerational sequel.

The truth is I wanted any excuse to get back to Ghost Lake.

When I wrote *The Maestro*, my family and I were visitors to the real "Ghost Lake" (I'm keeping the name a secret). We were guests of our good friends Geoff and Carolee Mason, to whom that book was dedicated. Since then, we've bought into a camp at the north end, and for the last umpteen years we've made it our home away from home, and not just during the summer. In fact, it was a trip one very snowy March that helped inspire this book. Survival takes on a whole new meaning in the winter, and I knew that any son of Burl Crow would be up to the task.

The tragedy at the heart of the story is based on a real incident that happened on the lake many years before my first visit. Most of a family drowned in an accident similar to the one I describe here. That said, let me be very clear that Dodge Hoebeek and his family are entirely fictional characters.

Do criminals really escape from jails by helicopter? Believe it or not, they do; that was the first impetus to write this story. Look it up.

For the purposes of this story, I have set two camps at the north end of Ghost Lake, but there are actually three, and one of them I commandeered for Nate to hide out in. Thank you, Janice and Michael Stephenson. Please excuse the "renovations" to your lovely camp, not to mention the mess. I know that Nate will clean it up spotlessly when he gets a chance — and fix that broken door.

The idea of sending a cell phone up in a drone to try to get reception was suggested by another Northender, Matt McLean. Thanks, Matt.

I have to thank Geoff Mason, yet again, for his wealth of knowledge about all things camp. Geoff read an early draft of this book, and I can assure you, dear reader, that anything in the book that looks wonky or just plain wrong falls on me.

And finally, I want to thank Amanda for that conversation on the back deck where you said, "Why not bring in the boating accident? How would that affect Nate?" Let's keep having those conversations on the back deck forever.